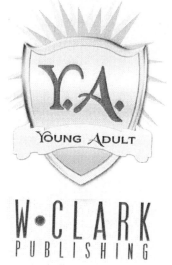

SADE'S SECRET

A SWEET 16 DIARIES NOVEL

BY

SPARKLE

Wahida Clark Presents Young Adult
60 Evergreen Place
Suite 904
East Orange, New Jersey 07018
973-678-9982
www.wclarkpublishing.com
www.wcpyoungadult.com

Sade's Secret
ISBN 13-digit 978-1936649433
ISBN 10-digit 1936649438
Library of Congress Catalog Number 2012905457
　　1.　Young Adult, Contemporary, Urban Fiction,
　　　　African American, – Fiction

Cover design by Nuance Art.*.
nuanceart@wclarkpublishing.com
Interior book design by Nuance Art
nuanceart@wclarkpublishing.com

Printed in United States
Green & Company Printing and Publishing, LLC
www.greenandcompany.biz

RAVE REVIEW

"Sparkle took me on an emotional ride within Sade's Secret. If I could have killed or maimed a person or two, I would have. The main subject matter was very strong and at times upsetting. Sade and Joyce's story provided a glimpse into the life of a mother depending on a man to provide her with all the love she needs, while sacrificing the sacred bond between a mother and her daughter. I recommend Sade's Secret to readers of family drama and mother-daughter relationships."

Jennifer Coissiere
Words Mosaic Review

ACKNOWLEDGEMENTS

First, I would like to thank God for not only the blessings, but also for the lessons as I continuously strive to be a better person.

I would like to thank my loving parents for the things they taught me and my two brothers. Although our paths went in different directions, you laid a solid foundation and for that, I'm thankful.

Thank you Wahida Clark for being a beacon of light in the publishing industry and open to sharing your knowledge with others. Thank you for this opportunity and I will forever be grateful.

To the best agent in the whole wide world, Dr. Maxine Thompson. Thanks for sticking with me through thick and thin.

To Andrew, thanks to you, I know what "real" love is.

For all of my literary divas and gents who are on this daily grind, see you in the trenches. A special shout out to everyone in All4One on Facebook.

Last, but not least, this book is dedicated to those who feel like they have no voice. You are not alone. Someone does care. Don't allow a negative situation to kill your dreams. There's someone out here cheering for you.

—Sparkle

~1~

SADE

Calvin, I need a hundred dollars to pay my dance fees." I said dressed in my black and white school uniform. I stood in the doorway to my mom and Calvin's bedroom with my hands on my hip.

With his disgusting crooked smile, he laid across the queen-sized bed and said, "Sade, call me daddy, and I'll think about giving it to you."

"What do you mean think about it? You told me last night that if I did what you wanted, you would give me the money this morning. I was supposed to have it last week, but mama don't get paid until Friday." I snapped throwing my long micro-braids behind my shoulder with attitude. Calvin was really pissing me off.

Since Calvin wanted to act like he was a pimp, he needed to pay up. "You're just like your mama, always got your hand out. You better be glad I'm a man of my word." Calvin rolled out of bed not bothering to cover up his tall muscular naked body.

Seeing Calvin naked wasn't anything new to me. I'd seen his peanut butter complexion more than I care to mention. Thinking about it, I couldn't remember why the smell or sight of the sticky paste that many people loved made me sick to my stomach...until now. I hated the fact that my mom had given him so much control over our household and it's been like that for the last five years. Although it took me awhile, I learned that since he was using my body for sex, I would use him for cash or other things I needed. Things that my mom couldn't afford to give me.

Calvin picked up his dingy, worn out wallet from the wooden dresser and retrieved five crisp twenty-dollar bills. He walked over to where I stood. "Can I get a kiss first?" I could smell his tart breath.

I held out my hand and rolled my pear shaped, dark brown eyes, not trying to mask my disgust. "I don't have time for this. Give me the money before I miss my bus."

Calvin handed me the money, but tried to sneak a kiss. Before his lips could land on mine, I turned and they landed on my chestnut brown cheek. I rushed to get away from him. I heard Calvin laugh from their bedroom doorway.

I grabbed my backpack off the floor and headed straight out the front door, bumping right into my mom. My mom worked the graveyard shift at least once a month at Dallas Metro Hospital. That's when

Calvin seemed to make his way to my room. He continued to violate me and I continued to remain silent because at this point, I felt as if it really didn't matter. No need to try to go against Joyce Washington. What she wanted, she got. Not knowing that I was paying the price for her decision to move her boyfriend in the house with us. She gave Calvin free reign of our household. At first, I was docile because I feared whippings. I still didn't want to obey Calvin and after getting so many whippings, I became immune to the pain. My mom figured that whipping me wasn't doing any good, so she finally stopped. It didn't stop her from fussing though.

I wished my mom would have dug a little deeper and realized why I disobeyed instead of jumping to the wrong conclusions, thinking I was just a mischievous child.

"Girl, you better hurry up and catch your bus because I'm too tired to drive you to school," Joyce snapped.

"I'm going, Mama." I walked down the apartment hallway that was filled with gang-affiliated graffiti.

I couldn't wait to graduate from Booker T. Washington so I could get away from Calvin and if truth be told, my mom too. Don't get me wrong, I love my mama, but sometimes she makes me so mad because how could she not see that her so-called perfect man was messing with me, her own daughter.

My pace slowed as I continued towards the bus stop. My mind drifted back to when my live-in nightmare all started. It was almost like a movie. Like I was watching on screen at the theatres as it happened to someone else, but it all happened to me.

Five years earlier...

"You know I love you, right," Calvin said as he got closer to me with his whiskey smelling breath.

My mom had been dating Calvin for less than a year. My mom trusted him enough to have him keep me while she was at work. But once he moved in, the kissing and touching started. I knew what he was doing wasn't right, but after every encounter, he assured me that he wouldn't do it again, but he would. He asked me not to tell my mama because she wouldn't understand. He made sure he gave me a dollar and candy after every encounter. Sadly, my silence would cost me. If I told my mom about the kissing and rubbing, then maybe, just maybe the horror that was about to occur wouldn't have happened.

Words escaped me, so I stayed silent. The moment Calvin's hands touched my body, I tensed up. That seemed to infuriate him. Instead of the sweet kind words he would usually whisper to me. He spouted out words that sent chills through my ten-year-old body.

SPARKLE

"Don't fight me on this Sade, because if you do, I will hurt you." The thirty-year-old six feet Calvin said as he stood over me.

The evil look in Calvin's cold black eyes put fear in my heart. I couldn't lose my mom. If I did, I would be all alone. I'd already lost my dad. I couldn't bear the thought of losing my mom too. My eyes bucked as I watched in horror Calvin unzipping his pants. I had never seen a man naked and the sight of Calvin's private part made me nauseous.

I had to get away, so I shot up in the bed and attempted to get up from under him. Calvin pushed me back down on the twin size bed and in a calm voice said, "Calm down, baby girl. You're going to like it as much as I will."

"No, Calvin. Please don't do this. I don't want to do it."

"Shhh." he said repeatedly as he used one of his hunds to force open my legs. Tears flowed down my cheeks while Calvin planted kisses on my face like I was the love of his life instead of his girlfriend's daughter. Terror filled my eyes when I felt Calvin ripping off my panties.

I squirmed underneath him, but it only seemed to make Calvin more excited because he verbally expressed his pleasure, so I stopped. Believing Calvin would hurt my mom, instead of screaming for help, I closed my eyes, did my best to block out what was happening by counting as Calvin violated my young body. The pain was unbearable so I screamed out in agony.

Would anyone hear my cries? Where was my mother? Why wasn't she home from work yet? Couldn't the neighbors hear? I asked these questions as I endured the assault to my body by my mom's boyfriend. The smell of Calvin's cheap old man soap and cologne filled my nostrils. I almost gagged on my own vomit.

Calvin finished his immoral act. With a sinister smile on his face, he said, barely above a whisper, "Not a word about this or I promise to kill you and your mama." Then in the next breath, he sounded like he was a concerned lover, "Sorry it hurt. It won't hurt as much next time."

The next time. Please, don't let there be a next time. I couldn't bear to look at him. Instead of responding, I whimpered.

Calvin kissed me on the forehead and rolled off the top of me. "That's a good girl. Remember, this little secret is between you and me. Joyce doesn't need to know."

My heart was beating so fast it felt like it was going to leap out of my chest. I held my breath not knowing what was going to happen next. Calvin turned around and said before leaving my bedroom, "Tomorrow, I'll see about getting you that doll you wanted."

SPARKLE

I didn't want a doll. I wanted what happened to erase itself from my memory. Soon as I heard Calvin close the bedroom door, I exhaled. My body ached from the abuse. I could barely open my legs and I felt a puddle of fluid on my sheets. I laid there without moving for an undisclosed amount of time.

The sound of my bedroom door opening caused my body to shiver. Please don't let it be Calvin coming back to do more damage, I said to myself. When I saw that it was my mother, I felt relieved.

My mom stood in the doorway in her hospital uniform. Instead of coming to my rescue, she yelled, "Sade, what's that smell? Get your nasty ass up and wash your behind. It don't make no sense for a little girl to be this nasty."

"Mama, it's not what you think," I said with tears running down my face not knowing exactly what to tell her.

She walked near my bed and saw the blood on the sheets. "Why didn't you tell me you started your period?"

"But, Mama..."

"But Mama nothing. Get up and clean yourself up. I got some pads under the sink and when you finish taking a bath, go wash those bloody sheets."

My mom wasn't making this easy for me. I felt ashamed. I wanted to tell her the blood wasn't from my period, but from what Calvin had done to me.

Fear stopped me from saying anything. Fear that Calvin would go through with his threat to harm my mom. I loved my mom and didn't want Calvin to hurt her, so I kept my mouth closed.

But maybe, just maybe, if my mom could look into my eyes, she would sense something and notice the hint that something tragic had just occurred. My body tensed up as I attempted to sit up in the bed.

"Girl, I don't have all day. Hurry up and get your bath so I can drop you off at school. I gotta come back and get me some sleep. You've been sleeping all night, while I've been on my feet cleaning behind sick people at the hospital."

I mustered up all the strength I could and got out of the bed. With the light now on, I knew my mom should see the pain in my eyes. Couldn't she see what my mouth couldn't say? Instead of showing compassion, the only look on my mom's face was a look of disgust as she turned up her nose at the funky smell that filled my small bedroom.

"Hurry up, girl. I told you I don't have all day." Without another word, Joyce headed out my bedroom door.

I wrapped my robe around my body, obeyed my mother, and followed behind her. Calvin stood near the bathroom door in the hallway as if he had been listening to see if I had busted him. When my mom stopped and gave Calvin a peck on the lips,

something inside of me screamed out in agony. How could my mom love such an evil man?

I eased by them in the hallway and went straight to the bathroom as tears flowed down my cheek.

Joyce said, "Girl, I don't know what's wrong with you this morning, but you need to hurry it up."

When I turned around in the direction of my mom's voice, I caught Calvin looking at me with his evil smile. He looked like the devil himself. I wished he would go away. I would never forget this day as long as I lived. My mom must have been blind. She acted like she didn't see the tears forming in my eyes. With me moving in slow motion, my mom didn't bother to ask me what was wrong. She was only concerned about hugging and kissing Calvin. How could she not know that her daughter had been violated in the worse way?

On that day, my innocence had been stolen, but little did I know it was just the beginning of my nightmare. It would be three more years before my menstrual cycle started and for the past five years, I held a secret; a secret that I've kept from everyone, including my two best friends: Crystal Jackson and Dena Bradford.

~2~

JOYCE

I watched from the apartment doorway as my only child walked down the hall. If Sade turned around, she would have seen the love on my face, but she never did. Tired, I closed the door and headed straight to the bathroom to take a long, hot shower.

As the water cascaded down my body, my mind thought back to happier times. Memories of Avery Washington, Sade's father, flashed in my mind. I couldn't help but smile as I thought about the love him and I shared. A love we shared that was so deep that only death could separate us. Tears flowed down my cheeks as I recalled that ill-fated day when a drunk driver stole from me the only man who truly loved me. On that day, a piece of me died, never to be resurrected. The little money I had saved went to bury my husband and at nineteen years old, I was now faced with raising a child by myself.

At the time, I felt fortunate to find a job at one of the local hospitals. It wasn't my ideal job, but I would do anything to keep a roof on top of our heads. The

government assistant I received was barely enough to keep diapers on Sade, let alone provide shelter, so I had no choice, but to find a job before we were homeless. Sadly, I had no family members to turn to. I rarely kept in touch with anyone and those that I did keep in contact with were all about themselves. Once I left Shreveport, Louisiana and moved to Dallas, Texas, it was like my family erased me from their memory. No one showed up for Avery's funeral to support me, even after I reached out to them. I knew then that I was in this world alone...my then nine-month old daughter and me.

I dried off and kept reminiscing about the past. The sounds of Calvin's snoring from the bedroom snapped me back into the present as I stood there in the bedroom doorway. Calvin's well-toned chest heaved up and down as I stared at him for a few minutes.

My head throbbed as I dealt with my own conflicting emotions. On one hand, I loved Calvin as much as I'm capable of loving a man after Avery, but on the other hand, sometimes the sight of him made me want to do him physical harm.

Calvin started being a good man to Sade and me, but over the last six years, he worked less and less and drank more and more. Calvin's favorite past time seemed to be hustling and gambling. The money he hustled, he lost gambling so he still wasn't contributing to our household the way he should have. Don't get me wrong, when he won big, he splurged on Sade and me, but that wasn't enough for me. I liked it when he had a steady job. It helped relieve some of my stress. Sometimes it felt like I was taking care of two children instead of one.

Funny how the thing that attracts you to a man can make you go crazy. Calvin's flawless complexion, ebony eyes, and baldhead made women drool. I knew women found him attractive, but since he was with me, I tried not to trip on the fact. Watching Calvin's well-toned body automatically made me look at my own. Calvin reminded me repeatedly about my aging and expanding body. I didn't need him to tell me that I was getting older and fatter. My tight fit clothes reminded me every day that I was packing on more pounds.

Every time Calvin would say, "Joyce, baby, I love you just the way you are, but you know a lot of men don't like their women fat," I would find myself believing his crap and stayed with him in spite of some of my reservations. Something about being alone frightened me.

I knew what Calvin was spitting was bull because my two close friends were several sizes larger than me and had no problems finding men who were attracted to their voluptuous bodies. If truth be told, men were always staring at my plump behind. I smiled because I know if I didn't have some junk in

my trunk, Calvin would have probably left me a long time ago.

Prior to meeting Calvin six years ago, it was hard finding a man willing to commit to me when they found out I had a child. They were willing to wine and dine me, but when I mentioned my daughter, they usually made excuses of not wanting the responsibility of raising some other man's child. Calvin was the only one who stayed around afterwards and that's one reason I have this strong allegiance to him. He accepted the fact that Sade and I were a package deal. Knowing that Calvin loved Sade was enough for me to stick it out through the good and bad times with him. Sade deserved a father figure in her life. I didn't have any control over what happened with her real father, but I did have a say so on what happened with Calvin. So regardless of the drama Calvin would sometimes put me through; I was determined to make it work with him.

Calvin must have sensed me watching him because he opened up his eyes and said, "Hey baby. Why don't you join me?"

"In a minute." I removed a pair of shorts and my Dallas Cowboys t-shirt from the dresser drawer. After placing them on, I slipped in the bed beside him. Calvin attempted to make a move on me, but I was tired and not in the mood for any hanky panky. "You need to brush your teeth." I avoided his kisses by turning over in the bed and placing my back towards him.

"You keep acting like that, I might have to find me another woman," Calvin said, in a non-joking manner.

"Whatever, Calvin. I'm sleepy. We can continue this when I wake up."

"I'll be gone when you wake up," Calvin responded.

I felt the bed move when he got out, but refused to turn around to face him. Instead, I mumbled, "I would be so lucky."

"What did you say?" Calvin asked.

"Calvin, please. Let me be so I can sleep." I shut my eyes tight, hoping Calvin would just leave.

"I'm tired of being ignored, Joyce. You better get it together or you're going to lose me for real."

On a mission to tune out Calvin's whining voice, I pulled the covers over my head. I exhaled as soon as I heard the door shut. I hated myself sometimes because I had become so dependent on Calvin. His sex game had me hooked. He was like a drug habit that I couldn't shake. As much as I claimed to be Ms. Independent, I just didn't have the willpower to leave him.

His charm, his sexy abs, and the way he made me feel kept me in our yo-yo relationship. If Calvin left on his own, I could possibly break the habit, but then

again, I would probably be miserable because in spite of his faults, he was the only man I had been with in so long.

I thought about what he said about losing him and I wasn't ready for that to happen so as tired as I was, I got out of bed. I could hear Calvin in the shower. I didn't want to risk losing him to another woman, so I did what any other woman would do to try to hold on to her man. I gave him the attention that he wanted. I took off my clothes, dropped them on the bathroom floor, and joined him in the shower.

An hour later, Calvin was retrieving money out of my purse, and I didn't care because sleep was calling my name. He walked to my side of the bed and kissed me on the cheek. "Baby, I'll be back by the time you wake up. I got a few things I want to do."

"Okay, baby," I responded, without questioning him. Calvin being happy was all that mattered to me. If he was happy, then I would be able to sleep peacefully.

I drifted off to sleep as Calvin walked out the front door to a destination unknown.

~3~

SADE

"Sade! Sade!" my fifteen-year-old best friend, Crystal, said several times to get my attention.

"What? I'm trying to get me some sleep." I rubbed my sleepy eyes and sat up in the bus seat.

"Ooh, were you on the phone with Rodrick all night?" Crystal asked.

"No. Just was up late last night. Wake me up when we get to school."

Rodrick was a senior who claimed he liked me and he wasn't afraid to let me know every chance he got. Truth be told, I liked him too, but I just wasn't ready for a serious relationship. My focus had been on keeping my grades up and singing. I had plans on being the next big star out of Dallas. People, especially boys, always said I had a body like Beyonce and everyone knew I could out sing Fantasia on any given day.

SPARKLE

I planned to use all of my assets to make it in the music business. I was thrilled when I was accepted into Booker T. Washington High School for Performing and Visual Arts. Several of my favorite singers, like Norah Jones and Erykah Badu graduated from Booker T. and I was determined to follow in their footsteps. Plus with a name like the famous singer, how can I not succeed?

Thinking of fame was the last thought in my mind before I drifted off into a light sleep. Just when the sleep was getting good, I felt a slight shake.

"We're here," Crystal said.

Still sleepy, I slowly grabbed my backpack and exited the bus behind Crystal. Dena waved at us and we walked in her direction. Out of us three, Dena was the shortest and people mistook her for being younger than what she really was because of her round baby face. We were all fifteen and were like the three musketeers.

Dena and Crystal were my best friends. We had been friends since elementary school. Although Dena's parents moved to another neighborhood several years ago, we kept in touch. We were thrilled when we all were accepted into the school that was known for its performing arts and academic program.

"What's up?" Dena asked, as we greeted each other with a hug.

"Would be fine if I wasn't so sleepy," I responded.

"Hope you don't fall asleep in Ms. Franks class again," Crystal said.

"Oh, I won't."

"Shorty, let me holla at you for a minute." At six feet two inches tall, seventeen-year-old Rodrick's skin was so smooth that it reminded me of a cup of milk chocolate cocoa.

I looked at Rodrick then back in Crystal and Dena's direction. "I'll catch up with y'all in class." I turned and faced Rodrick. "What's up?"

"You're what's up. When are you going to give me the pleasure of taking you out?" Rodrick said as he eased next to me, towering down at my mere five feet five inch frame.

"You know my mom won't allow me to date until I am sixteen," I responded, as we walked up the walkway towards the school.

"There's a school dance this Friday. Promise you'll be my date. Your mom won't have to know."

Rodrick, always a gentleman, held the front door opened and waited for me to walk in before following behind me.

"I'll think about it." I liked Rodrick, but I didn't want him to think I was easy. There were many girls of all races who would love to be in my shoes and hook up with him, but he seemed to be ignoring them because lately, he's been too busy trying to get with me.

Rodrick walked ahead of me and stopped. He was now blocking me from moving. His big brown eyes twinkled. "I promise to be on my best behavior."

I could feel my resistance wavering. "Okay. I'll meet you here Friday. I'd better not catch you up in some other chick's face either."

Rodrick smiled. "You've made me the happiest boy at Booker T."

"Yeah, yeah." I did my best to play it off, but I was excited about our upcoming date.

Rodrick walked me to class and we both were smiling from ear-to-ear. Dena and Crystal couldn't wait for me to sit down before trying to find out what happened with Rodrick and me.

"Shh," I said, not wanting everybody in my business as I slipped behind the desk in between them. "I'm going with Rodrick to the dance," I whispered.

Before either of them could ask for more details, our homeroom teacher walked in. Ms. Kravitz didn't play. Without Ms. Kravitz asking, we pulled out our English Literature book.

"You can put your books away," Ms. Kravitz said. "Today, you'll be taking a pop quiz. Let's see what you can remember about Native Son by Richard Wright."

"I'm screwed," Crystal said. "I haven't read it at all."

"Neither have I," Dena responded.

"Y'all can copy off my paper. I know this stuff like the back of my hand," I said with confidence.

Dena wiped her forehead. "You're a lifesaver."

Once again, I have to rescue my friends. They both looked at me to be the backbone and their strength when there were many days and nights I didn't feel like being strong for myself. Crystal and Dena were unaware that I knew a lot because reading and studying provided me a mental escape from the hell I endured at home being at the beck and call of Calvin, also known as the devil himself.

~4~
SADE

Friday couldn't come quick enough for me. The knee length tight black knitted dress hugged all of my curves. I admired myself in the full-length mirror nailed to the opposite end of my closet door. I turned to view myself at different angles. Not only would Rodrick's head turn when I entered the dance, so would the other guys.

"My, my, my. Looking good mamasita. Don't our little girl look good, baby," Calvin said as he stood in front of my bedroom door.

"I knew I should have kept my door shut," I mumbled.

Joyce walked up behind Calvin. "That dress is a little too short. You need to change."

Before I could protest, a knock was heard at the front door. "I don't have time. That's Crystal and her cousin Jada now."

Joyce gave me another look over. She walked up to me, tugged on the hem of the skirt, and pulled it. It stretched a few inches. "I guess it's alright. Where did you get the money to buy that anyway?"

"I borrowed it from Dena," I lied. I actually got the money from Calvin earlier during the week. I then snuck to one of the stores downtown and purchased it.

Calvin interrupted my thoughts. "Baby, let her go, so we can have us a little we time."

For once, I'm glad to hear Calvin intervene. "Thanks, Mom, for letting me go."

I gave my mom a hug and headed toward the front door.

"I want your behind back here no later than midnight. You hear me," Joyce said to me as she held the front door open.

Crystal stood on the other end of the door. "Hi, Ms. Joyce."

"Crystal, how are you dear? You look beautiful." Joyce cleared her throat. "See that's the kind of dress you should have worn."

Crystal's dress wasn't that much longer than mine was. It was just a different style. The red satin dress was flared at the end, but still accented Crystal's figure. With her auburn hair pent up, she looked like a younger version of the model Tyra Banks, including the height. The four-inch heels she wore accented her long lean legs.

"Oh mom." I rolled my eyes and said, "Come on Crystal."

"Midnight," Joyce yelled out as I rushed Crystal down the walkway.

"What's up with your mom?" Crystal asked.

"She's tripping."

Crystal said, "We got to wait on Jada to pick us up and you know she be on her own time. Plus, she knows about a house party, so I say we skip out of the dance around ten and head to it."

"I don't know about that," I said.

"Well, if you ain't down, you might as well stay home. 'Cause that's the plan."

We stopped a few feet away from where Jada was parked in her mom's black Ford Taurus.

I really wanted to hang out with Rodrick and my friends so staying at home wasn't an option. I shrugged my shoulders and responded, "Why not? My mom will never find out as long as I'm home by midnight."

"I'm sure if Jada can't get you home, somebody at the party should. Some more of my cousins should be there."

"Cool. I'm game."

"Let's go."

Crystal got in the front seat, while I eased into the back. After exchanging friendly chitchat, Jada blasted Lil' Wayne's latest CD all the way to Booker T. I tried to mask my nervousness. I was far from being confident. My palms sweated as I thought about meeting Rodrick at the dance for my first official date ever. Don't get it twisted. I've been to other school dances, but this was the first time I had an actual date.

"I'll be back to pick y'all up at ten. Be right here. Don't have me waiting," Jada said as Crystal and I exited the car.

"We'll be here," Crystal assured her.

I didn't have to look for Rodrick because as soon as Crystal and I walked into the dance auditorium, he walked up to me.

"You're the best looking chick here," Rodrick said as he leaned down and gave me a hug and kiss on the cheek.

The butterflies in my stomach danced around. At that moment, I felt like a million bucks and the luckiest girl at Booker T.

"What about me?" Crystal cleared her throat and asked with a huge smile on her face.

"You look good too, but Sade's my girl, so you know I only have eyes for her."

"Ooh, she got your nose wide open," Crystal teased.

"She sure does and I'm not ashamed to say it either." Rodrick reached down and grabbed my hand. "Follow me to our seat." He looked over at Crystal. "You too."

"I don't want to be a third wheel."

"Come on," I said. I was nervous and didn't want to be left alone with Rodrick. Having Crystal near would help me relax, or so I thought.

The deejay for the dance played all the latest tunes. "Would you like to dance?" Rodrick asked me when the latest Lil' Wayne song blasted through the place.

How could I resist Rodrick's big puppy-dog eyes? I allowed him to guide me to the dance floor and we danced on every song for the next hour. It wasn't until we returned to our seats that I noticed Dena was there.

Dena was in black leather pants, a matching halter top revealing her flat stomach, and black stilettos. If my mom thought the outfit I had on was too tight, I know for a fact she would never let me come out of the house wearing the "come get me" outfit Dena was wearing.

Rodrick said, "I'll be right back. I'm going to get us something to drink."

"Okay. I'll be right here," I responded, as I slipped in the seat next to Dena. "Girl, I love that outfit. You'll have to let me borrow it sometimes," I said.

"That big booty of yours would split this wide open."

"If your phat ass could fit in it, I know I can wear it too," I protested.

"We were blessed in that department, now weren't we?" We gave each other a high-five and laughed.

Several guys came up to our table, but I turned down all of their advances because Rodrick was the only guy I was interested in being with. Dena, however, decided to take one of the guys up on his offer and left me alone to go dance with a guy she had been having her eyes on all year.

I wondered what was taking Rodrick so long. He should have been back with our drinks by now. Tired of waiting, I got up and went in search of Rodrick. I scanned the room and to my surprise, Rodrick was holed up in the corner with another chick.

My blood pressure skyrocketed as I saw how intimate the two looked. "Oh, no he didn't. Don't nobody play Sade Washington."

Normally, I'm mild mannered. However, there were some lines you didn't cross and disrespect was one of them. I picked up a cup of punch off the table and made a beeline straight where Rodrick and the mysterious girl stood all cuddled up. When I got closer to where he stood, I called out, "Rodrick."

Apparently, he didn't hear me over the loud music so I got closer and yelled louder. "Rodrick."

He turned around and stuttered, "Sade, it's not what you think."

Maybe because of the sick relationship I had with Calvin, it made me very sensitive when it came to boys. The fact that Rodrick had made me put my

guards down and appeared to try to play with my emotions made me snap.

"Screw you Rodrick." I didn't wait for any other responses. I threw the drink from the cup in his face. Some of it splashed on the mysterious girl, who shrieked.

The girl yelled out obscenities and I left them both trying to clean up the mess.

~5~

JOYCE

ere I go again dealing with Calvin's shit. I paced back and forth in the living room. It was after eleven and Calvin was nowhere in sight. My attempts on calling Calvin's cell phone were unsuccessful. Each time I called his number, the phone call went straight to voice mail. I couldn't stand Calvin's best friend Mark. When I called him, he claimed to have a bad connection, but never called me back. I'm sure Mark knew exactly where Calvin was.

I probably should have been concerned about Sade's whereabouts since her curfew was quickly approaching, but right now; I'm concerned about my man and most importantly, whom he was with. This was supposed to be our date night. After Sade left for the dance, Calvin received a phone call and then made an excuse about having to go help out Mark with something.

I stopped and looked at myself in the bedroom mirror. Contrary to Calvin's complaints, I admitted to myself that I wasn't a bad looking woman. Yes, I'd

put on a few pounds over the years, but contrary to how Calvin tried to make me feel, men still approached me.

My insecurities had a way of making me think the worse about things. I'm sure most of the guys had ulterior motives, so I never took their advances seriously. Besides, Calvin was probably right. He was the only man who loved me. Flaws and all.

The thought of losing Calvin to another woman made me want to cry. We didn't have a fairytale relationship, but I loved him and knew he loved me too. There's no way I could lose him to another woman.

I stopped pacing the floor and rummaged through Calvin's dresser drawer. If I had to search through every drawer, I was determined to find something, anything, a clue to where he was. Bingo. I tore open one of Calvin's old cell phone bills. I skimmed the pages until I got to the page with the call logs on it. One number stood out. "Who the hell is this three four nine number? I hope this is not some woman's number because if it is, all hell's about to break loose up in this camp."

My eyes blurred as I noticed the same number dialed at odd times of the night. I clenched my teeth as I continued to scan the page.

"This is some bull," I yelled as I mentally compared the long night phone calls from the three four nine number to the times I worked the night shift.

I retrieved my cell phone from the dresser and used star six nine before dialing the number.

A female answered the phone. Now that I had her on the phone, *what should I say?* I thought. I remained silent.

"Hello," the female repeated herself.

If steam could exit my ears, they would. I was livid. "Let me speak to Calvin?" I didn't even pretend to be nice.

"Who is this?" the female asked.

"I'm his wife," I lied as I emphasized the word wife so there would be no misunderstandings on who I was to Calvin.

"Well, Calvin's not here. He just left. I suggest you call him on his cell phone." Without another word, the female hung up on me.

"No, that bitch didn't just hang up on me." Pissed, I dialed the number again. This time, the woman didn't answer. I wanted to punch something. Where the hell was Calvin and who in the hell was this woman? I called the number again.

The woman answered this time and said, "Look, I suggest you call your man and leave me out of this."

"The moment you slept with my man is the moment you got involved," I snapped.

"Calvin's not all that so you can have your man back," the woman responded and hung up on me a second time.

"You bastard. How could you?" I shouted. I cursed aloud while I removed Calvin's stuff out of the dresser and threw item after item on the floor. This was it. I can't take any more. I tried to hold on because I wanted Sade to have a father figure in her life, but enough was enough. I didn't stop until everything Calvin owned was in a pile in the living room or bedroom floor. By the time I finished wrecking havoc with his things, I was exhausted. Exhausted from the moving, crying, and yelling. All I could do at that point was fall on top of the bed. My eyes fell on the mess in the room.

"Joyce, what are you doing with my stuff?" Calvin asked when he arrived home and saw a trail of his clothes from the living room to the bedroom floor.

With bloodshot red eyes from crying, I looked him directly in his lying eyes. "I want you out of my house. How could you do this me? I've given you everything and cheating is how you repay me," Joyce said, barely above a whisper.

"Look. It's not what you think," Calvin stuttered. "What had happened was...that's one of Mark's women. She should have told you that." Calvin could barely look me in the eyes.

I laughed, although inside I felt like crying. "Do you think I'm a fool?"

"No, baby. I swear. I'm innocent this time," Calvin said with a straight face.

"I knew there was something going on. I just couldn't put my finger on it. You told me after the last time I caught you, that you wouldn't do it anymore."

"I'm not cheating on you, Joyce. I promise on five stacks of bibles." Calvin moved his hand to show me the height. He was pathetic.

Normally, Calvin was more defensive, got upset, and would curse, so maybe he was telling the truth. Maybe the woman was lying and I got things mixed up, I told myself.

Calvin walked through the trail of clothes and sat down on the bed next to me. He caressed my back as he talked. "You're enough woman for me. I don't need to mess with anyone else."

"Calvin, if I find out you're lying, it's over. I mean it this time," I said, between tears.

Calvin smiled. We both knew that I would still be there for him, regardless of what he did. Calvin had cheated numerous times before and each time I forgave him and never kicked him out.

With a smug look on his face, Calvin said, "Now clean this mess up, so when I get out the shower, I can show you how much I love you."

I watched Calvin walk away. He stumbled over the clothes as he made his way out of the room. I was in no mood to clean up the mess I made. I pushed all of his stuff to the side and into one pile and laid across the bed to wait for Calvin to return.

Whoever the mystery woman on the other end of the phone from earlier was now irrelevant because Calvin was here with me and would soon be in my bed.

~6~

SADE

I don't know what was in the punch this guy gave me, but it had me feeling tipsy. I should have known something was a little off when he kept insisting that I drink it. "I don't know what's in this, but it's good," I slurred.

Crystal seemed to come from nowhere and was all in my face. "Girl, I think you better leave the punch alone." Crystal fanned her hand. "That's why I don't like some house parties. Too much drinking and smoking going on for me."

"Party pooper," I said as Crystal led me away from the older guy who clearly was trying to take advantage of my drunken state.

"Your mama is going to kill you when she finds out you've been drinking."

"My mama's not going to find out because I'm not going to tell her."

"Come on, it's almost one and Jada's ready to go."

"Well, I'm not. I sort of liked what's his face."

"Sade, he's too old for you." Crystal continued to pull me towards the front door.

"He's only nineteen. I've been with older."

"Huh. What did you say? I thought you were a virgin?" Crystal asked.

I laughed. I guess I did have too much to drink. I stumbled alongside Crystal as we continued to walk through the crowd of people to the car. "I haven't been a virgin in so long."

"Well, you're my girl and I know for a fact that he's bad news."

"Rodrick's bad news too, so what. I sure know how to pick them."

Crystal asked, "So when did you lose your virginity?"

"Can we change the subject?" I asked. Crystal really knew how to spoil a night with her annoying questions.

Crystal helped me get into the back of Jada's car. Jada turned around and looked at her. "Hope your mama don't blame me for you being tore up."

I laughed. Crystal looked at me like I was crazy. Everything anyone said made me laugh. I couldn't help myself. I had the giggles. As Jada drove, I could feel every bump she hit as she dodged in and out of the late night Dallas traffic. My hand went to my stomach. "Ooh, I don't feel good."

"You better not throw up in my car is all I know," Jada yelled and looked at me in the rearview mirror.

Crystal said, "I think ol' dude spiked her drink with something. Good thing I saw what was going on because otherwise there's no telling what him and his friends would have tried to do."

I agreed and would have to thank Crystal letter, but for now, I had other things on my mind. "Pull over," I yelled.

Jada pulled over to the side of the road. I barely got the door open in time when all my insides seemed to pour out as I puked on the pavement.

Crystal yelled, "How gross?" Crystal passed me some tissue.

I took the tissue and wiped my mouth. I threw the tissue out, then got back fully in the car and closed the door.

Jada steered the car back on the road and continued towards our destination. First stop, my apartment complex. I rolled my eyes at Jada when she said, "Ewe. Crystal, give her a mint or something 'cause her breath smells foul."

I started to say something, but the pain in my stomach stopped me. I hoped we could make it home without me having to throw up again. With Jada's attitude, if I did have to throw up, I wouldn't even ask her to pull over. I would handle my business right

here in the backseat of her car. The thought of it gave me the giggles and I started laughing aloud.

Jada yelled, "What's so funny?" Jada looked at Crystal. "Your girl's drunk as I don't know what."

I had calmed down by the time we made it to my apartment. Apparently, Crystal wasn't too sure of my sobriety because she insisted on helping me out of the back of Jada's car when she stopped.

"I'll be right back," Crystal said as she helped me out of the car.

"We need to be real quiet. Hopefully, my mom will be sleep," I said as my giggles returned. I noticed as we walked up the walkway to the bricked apartment building how the wear and tear of the building seemed to show even through the moonlit night.

No matter how many times maintenance painted the walls in the hallway; some of the neighborhood kids would draw graffiti back on them. The artists were good, but some of the things they painted weren't attractive. They were more concerned about representing their gang affiliation.

As Crystal and I walked up, some of the neighborhood drug dealers whistled. "You need some help. I can help you get her home," one of the guys who was about our age said to Crystal.

"I got this," Crystal responded. Crystal turned to me, "I don't trust any of them so I'll get you to the front door, but afterwards, you're on your own,"

Crystal said as she continued up the stairs with me to my apartment.

"I'm alright. See." I moved my arm away from Crystal and attempted to walk a straight line. I almost fumbled over my own feet.

Crystal caught me just in time. "Go directly to your room when you get in and pretend that you're sleep if your mama comes in afterwards."

"Okay, Crystie. You're my bestest friend ever. I love youuu," I said.

"Shh. We're outside your door."

"Okey dokey. Bye Crystie." I gave Crystal a tight hug.

Crystal took my purse and got my keys out. She unlocked the door and said to me, "Remember what I said. Go straight to your room."

"Okay. I will." I walked in the apartment, shut the door, and secured the lock.

When my eyes adjusted to the semi-darkness, the light from the hallway shined enough light in the living room for me to see, I smiled. I smiled because there in the living room piled on the floor were Calvin's clothes. My mom finally woke up and saw Calvin for the devil that he was. He would be out of our hair and I could celebrate my freedom. Now things could get back to how they were before he came into our lives. I could get my mom back. I celebrated silently within my head.

SPARKLE

My mind was on celebrating as I stumbled towards my bedroom. I stopped dead in my tracks when I came face-to-face with the devil. What is he doing here? I wanted to scream. I thought my mom had finally come to her senses and kicked his ass out.

"Let me help you to your room. We wouldn't want to wake your mama up, now would we?" Calvin said, with an evil grin across his face.

I opened my mouth to protest, but nothing came out. It was like I was having an out of body experience as Calvin helped me to my room. My room wasn't big, but it was mine. I had a twin size bed with a pink comforter because pink was my favorite color. My walls were decorated with posters of Lil' Wayne, Drake, and Usher, among other celebrities I admired.

I wished one of them could save me. No, I screamed from the inside as he led me to the bed. "You shouldn't sleep in that," he stated.

"I'm okay." I fell back on top of the covers.

"No, you aren't. I can smell the alcohol and weed smoke on you and if I can smell it, your mama will be able to do so too."

Calvin was right, but I needed him to leave so I could get out of my clothes. *Why was he still here?* I thought to myself. Before I could react, he was helping me out of my clothes. It's like I was watching someone else as he not only removed mine, but his too.

"Calvin, please don't do this. I'm tired. I don't feel good," I protested.

"I know exactly how to make you feel good," he said as he ignored my plea.

I didn't have the energy to fight him off, so I became an unwilling, but willing participant as Calvin violated my body for an unnumbered time. Calvin was getting reckless because my mom was only a few feet away, I thought to myself as I drifted in and out of conscious.

~7~

JOYCE

The alarm buzzed at six o'clock on the dot waking me out of my sound sleep. Seeing Calvin next to me brought a smile to my face. Even though the alarm clock was loud, Calvin didn't stir. He could sleep through anything, I thought as I slipped out of bed so I could get dressed for work.

The mess from the previous night made me frown. I really didn't feel like cleaning it up so while I'm at work, I'll have Sade clean it up for me. I had been so wrapped up in the drama with Calvin; I forgot to check on Sade to see what time she made it home. Calvin had put it on me last night. I smiled as I thought about it. His love was so good and he had worked my body in so many positions that by the time we were through with our lovemaking, I slept like a baby.

During the night, I thought I heard moans coming from another part of the house, but after I determined it was a dream, I slipped back into a deep sleep and didn't wake up again until the alarm went off at six. After getting dressed, I looked in on Sade.

"That child sleeps so wild," I said to myself. "And she needs to start sleeping with clothes on too." I picked up the pink comforter off the floor and draped it on top of Sade's body. Sade stirred, but didn't wake up.

I kissed my girl on the forehead and then left out of the room, being careful not to slam the door. I forgot my keys so I returned to my bedroom. I paused for a moment while in the doorway and watched Calvin sleep.

"I love you so much, Calvin. Please don't mess up what we have by sleeping with another woman. I don't know how much more of this I can take."

I grabbed my keys off the nightstand and then headed to work. After working my ten-hour shift, I returned home and the same clothes that were thrown in the living room the night before was still there.

"Sade!" I yelled.

"What?" Sade yelled back.

"Girl, don't 'what' me. Why didn't you clean up the living room like I told you?" I made a straight beeline to her room.

Sade was underneath her pink comforter almost in the same position I left her this morning.

"I'm not feeling well. I've been in bed all day," Sade responded.

"Well, what's wrong with you?" I asked. Maybe I shouldn't be so hard on her because she did look a hot mess. Sade's eyes were puffy, but I still couldn't tell from looking at her what was wrong.

"I don't know. I've been feeling like this all day."

"You should have said something when I called you earlier." Sade could be so elusive with me at times. I don't know if it's because of her being a teenager or what.

"I did, but you had already hung up."

"Child, well, get yourself together. I'll be in your room to check on you." I left Sade alone and headed to my bedroom.

Calvin was nowhere in sight. I was on the verge of getting upset. The only thing that stopped my blood pressure from rising was the fact that I noticed he had cleaned up our bedroom. Too bad he hadn't done the same for the living room.

I retrieved the cordless phone from the cradle and dialed Calvin's cell number, but not to my surprise, his phone went to voice mail.

I would deal with Calvin later. I need to take care of that mess in the living room. Just because we lived in the projects, didn't mean my apartment had to resemble the outside. I worked hard to ensure that we had nice things within my apartment. No, my furniture was no longer new, but it was mine and I kept it in good condition. I hated a messy apartment, but because I caused the mess and Sade was sick, as tired as I was from my ten-hour shift, I cleaned up.

I called Calvin again after cleaning up the living room and still no answer. Frustrated, I got out of my work clothes and showered to help release some of the tension.

I was surprised to see Calvin waiting for me in the bedroom.

"Hey, baby," Calvin said as he greeted me with a hug and kiss.

The tension that I had released in the shower immediately took over my body. "I called you," I snapped.

"I know. Didn't call you back because I was right around the corner from the house," Calvin responded.

With a raised eyebrow, I responded, "Uh. Okay."

"Come on now. Don't be having an attitude with me. I'm home, ain't I?"

I rolled my eyes. I really wasn't in the mood. I hoped this wasn't going to be a repeat of the night before. "Whatever, Calvin. You need to answer your phone when I call. You don't know why I was calling."

"Well, I figured if it was an emergency, you would have called me back," he responded.

"Why didn't you tell me Sade wasn't feeling well?"

"You know I don't be all up in her business like that," Calvin snapped.

"Well, y'all in the same house. You hadn't seen her today so you should have checked in on her." I walked passed him to the closet so I could get my clothes and get dressed.

"I'm not a babysitter."

"I thought you loved Sade."

"I do, baby. I do. I love Sade just as much as I love you." Calvin walked up behind me and hugged me tight.

"Well, I want you to act like it and act more concerned about her." I closed my eyes and enjoyed the feel of Calvin's tight embrace.

"Anything for you, baby," Calvin responded.

Sade was almost sixteen so she would be all right, I told myself as I spent the rest of the evening hugged up with Calvin in bed.

~8~

SADE

I spent the majority of the weekend over the toilet. The spiked punch from Friday night did a number on my stomach. After this terrible weekend, I would never ever take another drink again. Before I laid down again, I got up and removed my diary from under my mattress. My hand ran across the pink cover I had made before I opened it up to write about this past weekend's events. My phone rang several times, but I ignored the calls as I expressed my thoughts on what I called the secret pages of my life.

I once saw on a talk show that writing about your thoughts will help you cope with your life situations. With all I had going on, I needed to be able to express myself. Writing in my diary helped me cope.

My phone rang again. Since I didn't have anything else to write about, I put my diary to the side and answered. The call went to voice mail before I could

answer. I scrolled through my call log and saw several missed calls from Rodrick, Crystal, and Dena. Rodrick could kick rocks. Every time I heard his voice on my voicemail, I hit the seven button and erased them.

After clearing out my messages, I dialed Crystal's number. After exchanging pleasantries, I said, "Thanks for checking on me. I'm all right. Just been throwing up all weekend."

"Dena and I were worried about you. I told her about what happened Friday after we left the dance."

"I'll call her in a minute."

"So, you're going to be at school tomorrow?" Crystal asked.

"I plan on it. I haven't picked up a book all weekend so I hope we don't have any pop quizzes."

"What you going to do about Rodrick?"

"Nothing. Rodrick can kiss my butt. I've watched my mom deal with a no good man and I'm not going to put up with one."

"I know that's right. My mama and dad fight so much, I don't know why they are even together," Crystal said.

"At least you have both of your parents. I never got to know my dad." I tried not to sound jealous as I pouted.

"Sorry, I didn't mean to make you feel bad."

"Oh, girl. It's not your fault my dad's no longer here. I wish he was and maybe, just maybe, things would be different."

"You know Friday night; you mentioned you weren't a virgin. What's that all about?" Crystal asked.

I squirmed in my seat. I didn't want to divulge why I'm no longer a virgin to Crystal. I didn't want her to think less of me. I know the relationship with Calvin was sick, but it's hard for me to bring myself to say anything to anyone about it; especially to Crystal or Dena.

"I was a little tipsy. I don't know what I was talking about," I lied.

"Well, my mom says people say what they really mean when they are drunk so spill it. I want all the juicy details."

Since Crystal was not going to let up, I decided to give her the juicy details that she wanted. I picked up one of the romance books I had stolen from my mom's bookshelf and read a passage from it, giving Crystal a blow by blow of what happened. It sounded so believable; I almost believed the story myself.

"Wow. So who was he? Is he one of the guys from the neighborhood? Why aren't you with him now?" Crystal asked question after question.

"He was visiting his grandmother for the summer, but went back home. I haven't heard from him since, but it's cool."

"I would be freaking out. At least you got it over with. Me. I still haven't met a guy I love yet."

"If I were you, I would wait until you were married."

"But you didn't," Crystal said.

"I wish I could have." If only Crystal knew the truth. If only I had a choice, but Calvin took my choice away.

"You had a choice, but you chose to do it with that guy."

"I really didn't have a choice, but hey, let's change the subject. We need to start our group. We can sing and Dena can rap. We could be the new age Destiny's Child."

"I'm down. I'm sure Dena will be too," Crystal responded.

"Cool. Because I'm tired of living like this. There's a showcase coming up. I think we need to enter it. The only problem is how are going to come up with the two hundred and fifty dollar entry fee?"

"Get Dena on three way," Crystal said.

A few seconds later, we were all on the same call. "Girl, you over there acting like you grown and things," Dena teased me.

"Might as well be. My mom barely has time for me. When she ain't working, she all up under him." I just couldn't understand my mom sometimes. I mean she said she loved me, but she's been spending most of her free time with Calvin. Calvin's a grown man. I'm the one that needed her attention.

"I still don't know why you don't like Mr. Calvin. He seems nice to me," Dena said.

Crystal said, "He seems creepy to me."

"I don't want to talk about Calvin. We have more important things to discuss." I repeated to Dena our idea of entering the showcase.

Crystal said, "What should we call ourselves?"

"Something dealing with love," Dena responded.

"I got it." I picked up my diary and turned to an entry where I talked about wanting my own singing group. I read the big bold letters aloud to Crystal and Dena. "Adore. Let's call ourselves, Adore."

"Adore," Crystal repeated. "I don't know."

"I like it." Dena repeated the words "Adore" repeatedly.

Crystal sounded reluctant at first, but agreed. "We can go with Adore," Crystal said.

Dena responded, "I'm down. Oh and I got the money for the entry, but you all have to buy your own outfits."

Crystal said, "Where did you get that kind of money?"

"My mama gave it to me," Dena responded.

"My mom's too busy giving all of her money to Calvin," I blurted out, not caring about airing my family's business.

"Sade, get off that phone and come here," Joyce yelled from the other side of my door.

"Oops. She might have heard me. I got to go." I hung up the phone without waiting on Crystal or Dena's response.

I eased off the bed and opened the door. To my surprise, my mom wasn't outside my door. I did, however, locate her sitting in the living room on the couch. "Yes mom."

"Calvin and I had a talk. He told me that you've been sassing back at him. You know he's the only daddy you've had since your own father died, so you must show him a little more respect."

I had to blink my eyes a few times because why was my mom trying to check me about Calvin? "I don't say anything to Calvin, unless he says something to me, so I don't know what he's talking about."

"Well, I just want to make sure you don't be getting smart with him. You know you have a smart mouth."

"But..." I protested.

"No buts. Calvin's been like a father to you and from now on, you need to make sure you act like it."

I blurted out, "He's not my father," but really wanted to say, "No father of mine would do what he does."

"Watch your tone, young lady. I can still lay you out."

I couldn't look at my mom. "Mom, I'm sorry. I'll never think of Calvin like a father and there's nothing you can do to make me feel differently."

"Please try. For me."

"Mom. It's not going to happen. Can I be excused now?" I asked.

"Sure. But just watch your mouth. At least show him that much respect."

"Whatever," I mumbled as I walked away. I knew enough to say it low. If my mom heard me, I didn't want to chance her following through with her threat and hitting me. No indeed. I didn't need a knot upside my head.

~9~

JOYCE

W here's Sade?" I asked Calvin as I slipped in the bed beside him after another long twelve-hour shift at work.

He rubbed his sleepy eyes. "She's not in her room? She was there when I went to bed."

As tired as I was, I got out of bed and went to Sade's room to check on her. Sade was not there. Where could she be? I asked myself as I rushed to get the phone so I could call her. I was pressing the last digit of her phone number when the front door swung open. Sade walked in like she didn't have a care in the world.

"Where the hell have you been? I've been worried about you," I yelled.

"I was at Crystal's. I fell asleep and her cousin Jada just dropped me off."

"You better not be out there with some nappy headed boy messing around. I'm telling you if you come up in here with a baby, you and that baby are on

53

your own. You're my only child and the only one I plan on raising."

"I wasn't with a boy," Sade tried to assure me. "I was with Crystal. If you don't believe me, call her."

"Next time, let somebody know where you're going."

"Yes ma'am." Sade left me standing in the living room by myself.

Relieved that Sade was safe and secure, I went to bed and slept throughout the night. The next morning, Calvin surprised me with breakfast in bed.

"I knew you would be too tired to cook, so I cooked some of your favorites. Plus there's something I want to talk to you about."

Calvin handed me the tray. The plate was filled with sausage, scrambled eggs, grits, and toast. After eating the breakfast, I wouldn't be good for nothing, but going back to sleep.

"Must be serious if you're cooking," I teased, after taking a sip of orange juice.

"You'll find out soon enough. But I'm not going to do it this morning. You're off today, so I want you to go get your hair and nails done and tonight, I'll take you and Sade out for dinner."

"With whose money? You know we can't afford to be going out," I responded.

Calvin placed two hundred dollars on top of the tray. "My odd jobs have been paying off. Is there

anything wrong with me wanting to do something for my baby?" Calvin asked.

I thought about it. It would be great to be able to go to a salon to get my hair done. I'm tired of penny pinching and beyond tired of relaxing my own hair. "Do you have enough for Sade to get her hair done?" I asked.

"No, baby. Well, here's twenty dollars. Get her a boxed perm. You can do it when you get the time."

Calvin peeled off twenty dollars from his money clip and placed it on the tray. He bent down, kissed me on the forehead, and left out of our bedroom.

While Sade was in school and Calvin was out doing God knows what, I went straight to my favorite beauty salon and got my hair and nails done. With my fresh perm and new haircut, I felt like a million bucks. I don't know what kind of odd jobs Calvin's doing, but I'm happy he gave me the money. It's been awhile since he's given me extra money that didn't go towards any bills.

Calvin had never had a steady job, but always had money, until the past year. All of his odd jobs lately barely paid him enough to buy groceries. He used his money to stock up on cigarettes and keep his cell phone on. I hate to admit it, but I've gotten used to being the breadwinner. I worked overtime if that's what it took to keep a roof over our heads and food on the table. Rarely did I have extra money over to treat myself to get my hair and nails done. On occasion, I would sacrifice and get Sade's hair done. She got braids so that would only be once every three months.

A part of me felt guilty for not sharing some of the money Calvin gave me with Sade. But today, I needed a pick me up. What woman didn't feel better after getting her hair done? I was looking good too. Now, maybe, just maybe, I wouldn't have to worry about Calvin straying elsewhere. I eyed myself in the bathroom mirror again. I was confident that Calvin would love my new look.

"Mama," Sade yelled out.

"I'm in the bathroom," I responded. "I'll be out in a minute."

I walked in the living room.

"I love your hair, mama," Sade said as soon as she saw me. "It makes you look younger."

"You think so?" My hand automatically went up to stroking my black straight hair that had a lot of body.

"You look good. Real good, mom."

I couldn't help but beam with pride. It had been a long time since I felt beautiful. I had Calvin to thank for that, I thought, but quickly pushed the thought out of my mind.

"Dear, I wish I would have had enough to get your hair done, but Calvin only gave me enough for me. But when I get paid, I promise to get your hair done,

okay, sweetie." Guilt had me apologizing to Sade. I knew I was rambling.

"Cool. Jada knows how to braid hair and she'll do it for seventy-five dollars if I just buy the hair," Sade responded. "I'll need two bags of hair and that's about twenty-five dollars."

"Tell her, you want it done next weekend."

I hope I wasn't over extending myself, but I made a promise to Sade so even if I had to work overtime to make it up on the next check, I would. Maybe, Sade and my relationship could get back to where it used to be five years ago.

~10~

SADE

I was glad to see my mom in such a good mood. I couldn't remember the last time I'd seen my mom excited about anything. Ever since Calvin had been in our lives, I felt like I was losing my mom to him. Today, my mom's attitude reminded me of how things used to be. Pre-Calvin days.

I looked in the mirror as I brushed my hair back and put it in a ponytail. I wished we were going to dinner by ourselves. I wished Calvin would disappear out of our lives. That would be perfect, but life hadn't been perfect for me for some time.

"Dear, are you almost ready? Calvin and I are waiting?" my mom said from the other side of the bathroom door.

"I'm coming," I responded. A sharp pain shot through my stomach. I felt the food I had eaten earlier rise through my body. I barely made it to the toilet in time as it released itself splashing in the toilet.

Every time I got up, more puke would rise. After about ten minutes, I got up, washed out my mouth, and exited the bathroom. "Sorry for taking so long. Maybe you two should go by yourselves. My stomach's hurting."

My mom walked up to me and placed the back of her hand on my forehead. "You don't feel like you have a fever. Maybe you're coming down with one of those twenty-four-hour viruses." Joyce looked at Calvin. "Maybe we should order in and go out another time."

Calvin said, "Sade, do you think you're well enough to stay by yourself because I have something really important to talk to your mom about tonight?"

I gritted my teeth. My mom looked so beautiful. I didn't want to spoil her night, so I responded, "I'll be fine, mom. Go and have a good time."

"You sure? Because Calvin and I can go out another time."

"I'm positive. I'll be fine. I'll just lay down for a bit and it'll probably go away," I assured her.

"Okay, baby girl," my mom said as she hugged me.

I watched them leave the apartment. My mind was on my body. Something strange was going on. It had been out of sorts ever since I drank at that party. I don't know what kind of drug was in it, but it had to be something, because every time I turned around, I was feeling bad.

I could have told my mom, but then she would have asked me too many questions; besides dealing with Calvin was enough. I didn't need her worrying about me. I went back to my room and called Dena on the phone. "Dena, I need you to log on to the internet and find out what I have. I'll give you my symptoms and you tell me what it says on the internet."

Dena obliged by listening to me spurt out how I felt. Dena was unusually quiet, so I asked, "Dena, are you getting all of this?" just in case the call had dropped.

Dena responded, "I don't need the internet to tell you what's wrong with you. I think I already know."

"Well, spill it because I need to get me some medicine 'cause I'm tired of feeling like this."

"Sade, my friend, you are pregnant."

"Preg--what!" I yelled. Good thing I was home alone because I yelled loud enough for anyone within the apartment to hear me.

"From what you're telling me, you have the symptoms of being pregnant. When was your last menstrual cycle?"

I scanned my memory bank and couldn't remember. In fact, it had been a couple of months since I recalled having a period. "Ugh. At least two months, I think."

"Oh my. Wait until Crystal finds this out. She told me you said you weren't a virgin anymore. Wow. Did you not think about protection?" Dena asked.

I heard Dena talking, but my mind was stuck on the fact that I could be pregnant. This couldn't be happening to me. If I were pregnant, what would I do? There was no doubt that Calvin was the father. He was the only man I had been with in that way. Tears flowed down my face as I thought about how my life went from being bad to a living nightmare.

"What am I going to do?" I repeated between tears.

Dena said, "I'm on my way over there. I'll bring a pregnancy test, so we can confirm for sure."

I held the phone because I was in a state of shock. Pregnant. Me. At fifteen years old. I couldn't be. Or could I? Less than an hour later, Dena was knocking at the door carrying a bag. She grabbed my hand. "Come on so we can see if you're pregnant."

I followed Dena into the bathroom. She removed a stick from the plastic and handed it to me. "What am I supposed to do with this?" I held the stick and looked at it at several angles.

"Pee on it. Then if it's blue and straight, you're not pregnant. If it comes back with a pink positive sign, you are."

"Fine. I don't think I am, but if you insist, I'll do it."

Dena left the bathroom and shut the door. I took the stick and held it under me as I peed on it. I placed it on top of the box, washed my hands, and opened the bathroom door.

"It's done. Now how long do we have to wait?"

"We should know something in a few minutes," Dena said.

I started to ask Dena how she knew so much about taking a pregnancy test, but didn't. I was too scared of the results. My life could change within a matter of seconds. I picked up the stick, but closed my eyes. I handed it to Dena. "I can't look. You tell me."

Dena grabbed the stick and then looked at me. I could tell from her expression that it was positive. I took it from her and just as Dena suspected, I was indeed pregnant.

I rocked back and forth. "Dena, what am I going to do? I can't be pregnant. I just can't be."

Dena wrapped her arm around my shoulder. "It's going to be okay, Sade. You have me. You have Crystal. We'll be here when you tell your mom, if you want us to be."

"I can't tell her. It's going to kill her."

Dena said, "You have to tell her. This is something you won't be able to hide for long."

"I don't know. Maybe, maybe I should get rid of it." What Dena didn't know was that Calvin was my baby's daddy and having this baby could complicate things. Getting rid of it was something I would have to consider.

"First, you need to talk to your mom. You need to talk to the father of the baby and see what he wants to do."

"Forget the father. This is my body and I'm going to be the one to decide whether or not I keep this baby." I didn't mean to sound so harsh, but Dena didn't know the facts so her advice wasn't right for me.

"I'm on your side, remember? Calm down." Dena patted me on the back as an attempt to calm me down.

Dena eventually left, leaving me alone to face the fact that I was pregnant with the devil's child. Should I abort it or keep it? So many questions went through my head. Would God forgive me if I aborted Calvin's baby? Regardless, one thing I know I must do is finally tell my mom about her beloved boyfriend. I made up my mind that I would do so tonight. Tonight would be the night my mom would find out what Calvin had been doing to me all of these years.

~11~

JOYCE

The ambiance of the restaurant set up the stage for a romantic and relaxing evening. I was sort of glad that Sade didn't come with us tonight. It gave Calvin and me a chance to be with one another outside of the apartment.

Calvin looked so handsome sitting across the table from me. The smile on his face seemed to brighten up the room. "Joyce, I know I've put you through some things over the years, but you've stood by me. No man could ask for more from their woman. I love you so much."

"I love you too," I responded to Calvin, as I gazed into his eyes.

Calvin got out of his chair and got down on one knee in front of me. Other people in the restaurant started looking in our direction. His actions caught me totally off guard. "Calvin, what are you doing?"

Calvin ignored my question. He opened up a black velvet box and inside was a small diamond ring. This

was coming as a total surprise to me. The ring was small, but I didn't care about the size because the man I loved was kneeling before me with love in his eyes. I wiped the tears that formed in the corner of my eyes. I could feel my heart beat increase as I waited to hear the words that hadn't been spoken to me since Avery proposed to me over sixteen years ago.

Calvin took the ring out of the box and reached for my hand. "Joyce, would you do me the honor. Will you marry me?"

Before he could get everything out, I blurted out, "Yes, Calvin. Yes."

People around us clapped. I held my hand out as Calvin placed the ring on my finger. Calvin stood up and gave me a kiss on the lips. I looked at the ring and then back at Calvin as he took a seat back in the chair on the opposite side of the table. "You've made me the happiest woman in the world tonight."

"I plan on making you happy for the rest of our lives," Calvin said.

"Wait until we get home and tell Sade. I can't eat another bite. I'm too excited." I couldn't keep my eyes off my ring. Yes, the diamond was small, but it was cute and it was a token of my man's love for me.

"You sure you don't want dessert?" Calvin asked.

"No, baby. This ring was all the dessert I needed."

Calvin smiled. "Well, I have another surprise for you too. Call Sade and tell her to lock up everything.

Tonight, my dear. We're spending the night at the Omni."

"Oh my goodness. Did you win the Texas state lottery or something? First the hair, dinner, the ring and then a night at the Omni? Don't wake me up if I'm dreaming." It had been a very long time since I had been this happy.

I pulled out my phone and called Sade as instructed. "Baby, lock up. We won't be back until tomorrow."

"There's something I need to talk to you about," Sade said.

"Can it wait until tomorrow?" I asked, not once taking my eyes off my fiancé. Sade didn't say anything so I asked, "Sade, are you there?"

"I guess it can wait," Sade responded, before hanging up.

Sade sounded a little disappointed, but I refused to let it rain on my parade. I was happy and no one was going to threaten my happiness today. The man who I've dedicated the last six years of my life to had made it official. We were officially engaged.

Calvin paid our bill and I glowed with excitement as I followed Calvin out of the restaurant. We enjoyed a night of bliss in our hotel room, but unfortunately returned to the real world around noon the next day. Sade was at school so we were home alone. I couldn't wait for her to get home from school so I could tell

her the good news. I started to send her a text message, but decided to wait to tell her in person.

With so much positive energy flowing through my body, I decided to give the apartment a thorough cleaning. The kitchen, although small was big enough for a small kitchen table. The wallpaper in the kitchen needed to be replaced and it would have been nice to have new cabinets, but I made due with what I had and cleaned up the counters and swept the floor.

It didn't take me too long to clean the living room. I was glad I convinced the apartment manager to pull up the mangy carpet so that I could have hardwood floors. It was better than trying to vacuum a stained carpet that the apartment folks wouldn't replace. I saved the bathroom for last.

I put on some gloves as I prepared to clean the toilet. I placed some of the paper towels in the trash bag, but something caught my eye. I reached my gloved hand into the trash and pulled out a pink E.P.T. pregnancy test box.

"What in the world?" I caught myself saying aloud. "Oh, my goodness. My baby might be pregnant."

I reached back in the trash to look for the stick to confirm, but didn't see it. I rushed to Sade's room and the evidence I was looking for was staring me straight in the face. The white stick with a pink positive sign stared right back at me.

"Mom, what are you doing?"

"I guess I should be asking you," I responded, as I turned around holding the stick with the positive pink sign.

"Give me a minute and I'll explain everything."

"Yes. Please do." I counted backwards from twenty to calm my nerves. I would hear Sade out before pouncing on her for getting pregnant. "Eighteen... seventeen ...sixteen ..."

"Is Calvin here?" Sade asked, as she placed her backpack on the floor in front of her bed.

I forgot about counting and blurted out, "No, thank God because I don't need him hearing what I'm about to say to you. I never thought a daughter of mine would disappoint me the way that you have."

"Mama, hear me out." Sade said as tears flowed down her cheeks.

Sade's crocodile tears were not going to work. I waved the stick around and continued on with my rant. "This here confirms you're pregnant. If you wanted to screw around, you should have come to me and I could have put you on some form of birth control."

"But, mama, it was never my intention to get pregnant."

"If you have sex, there's a one hundred percent chance you will get pregnant. You should have come to me and we could have talked about it."

"It's not what you think. I didn't know how to tell you." Sade held her head down in shame.

"Now it's too late. You're a little girl yourself. How are you going to raise a child?" The more I thought about this situation, the angrier I got at not only Sade, but at myself. I saw how her hips had spread, but I thought it was because of good eating not because she was having sex.

"I can get an abortion," Sade blurted out.

"Oh no. No child of mine will be getting an abortion. You should have thought about the consequences before gapping your legs open. Who's the daddy? I need to talk to him as soon as possible?"

"Mom, maybe you should sit down for this," Sade said.

"Baby girl, what you need to do is tell me who the daddy of this baby is so I can talk to his parents and see what they plan on doing for this child of yours."

Sade wiped the tears from her eyes and looked me directly in my eyes. In a low raspy voice, Sade said, "Mama, the baby's daddy is Calvin."

"Oh, so you've been seeing a Calvin too."

"No, mom."

It was beginning to register to me what Sade was saying. My legs wobbled, but I didn't sit. I stood directly in front of Sade and dared her to lie to me. "Tell me again, who is the daddy?"

Sade repeated slowly, "Your man, Calvin."

Before I knew it, my hand drew back and I slapped Sade. Sade's hand flew to her right cheek and tears streamed down Sade's face.

She could stop with the tears. I held my hand up. "See this."

Sade sniffled, but didn't say anything.

I pointed at my engagement ring and yelled, "Calvin just proposed to me. We're getting married. You must have known about it."

Sade stuttered, "I had no idea you were getting married."

"I don't believe you. Fess up. What you're trying to do is not going to work." Sade was pissing me off more and more with her lies. I grabbed her by the shoulders and shook her. "You need to tell me who the daddy is so we can get all of this straightened out."

Tears returned to Sade's eyes and she sobbed uncontrollably, "Mama, Calvin's been sleeping with me since I was ten years old. I was too scared to tell you."

I blinked a few times. Yes, this was my daughter in front of me, but she must be an imposter. This couldn't be my daughter. No daughter of mine would say what she just said about the man I'm about to marry. The man that I've loved for the past five or six years would never do something as horrible as what Sade was accusing him of.

SPARKLE

I knew Sade had problems with Calvin, but I never thought Sade would go to this extent to break us up. Was Sade even pregnant? Was Sade trying to set this up the whole time? So many questions ran through my mind as I stared at Sade as she spurted out the same lie about Calvin being the father of her unborn child. I pinched myself because I must be sleepwalking. I must have dozed off between cleaning the rooms. This had to be a nightmare.

"Mama, I'm not lying. Calvin's my baby's daddy," Sade said again.

Sade's words vibrated in my head as I pushed Sade back on the bed and walked out of the room like a zombie.

~12~

SADE

As soon as my mom left out of the room, I fell on my bed crying. I thought my mom would be outraged at what Calvin had done to me, but instead she thought I was making it all up.

How could she not believe me? I'm her daughter. I wouldn't lie about something as serious as this. Anger swept through my body and dried my tears. I got out of bed and went to confront my mom.

My mom sat on the edge of her bed in a daze. I stood for a few seconds to see if she was going to acknowledge me, but she didn't. Upset, I blurted out, "All these years I've held on to this secret and now that I'm telling you mom. You act like I'm lying. Well, I'm not lying and I'm not holding on to the secret anymore."

My mom refused to look at me as she spoke. "You will not disrespect Calvin again. You hear me? Don't tell nobody else what you told me."

I refused to go away quietly. I had remained quiet for five years too long. I walked over to her dresser

and with one huge swipe, used my arms, and made everything on the dresser fall to the floor.

My mom looked at me with a crazy look and yelled, "Sade! You better get down there and clean up that mess."

"I'm not doing shit."

"If you don't clean up."

I interrupted her. "What mom? What more can be done? Your no good boyfriend. Correction, fiancé has been screwing your daughter and you act like you don't give a damn."

"I do care. Stop saying that. But you're lying and I will not have you spreading those lies about Calvin."

I rushed to my mom's bedside and fell to my knees. I grabbed her hand and pled, "You got to believe me. I wouldn't lie about nothing like this."

"What's going on here?" Calvin asked, as he walked in their bedroom.

"Nothing baby," Joyce said as she wiped her damp face. "Get up Sade. This conversation is over."

I couldn't believe it. My mom was actually ignoring everything I told her. I got up off the floor. I looked at her and then at Calvin. I looked down at my mom and with pain in my heart said, "I hate you. I hate both of you."

As I stormed out the room, I heard Calvin ask my mom, "What's that all about?"

She responded, "Nothing. She's just going through something."

I could hardly breathe. I had to catch my breath. My chest heaved up and down. I felt like I was having a panic attack. I needed air. I needed something. I needed to talk to my best friends. I plopped on my bed and got Dena and Crystal on a three way call.

Neither Crystal nor Dena said anything as I told them everything. I felt like the weight of the world was lifted off my shoulders.

Crystal's the first one to speak. "Sade, why didn't you tell us? We're your best friends and you kept a secret like this from us."

"Yes. We're supposed to be your girls," Dena added.

I didn't have an answer for their concerns. Maybe telling them Calvin was the father wasn't such a good idea after all. Maybe I should have kept what happened to me a secret. I couldn't control the tears that now ran down my face.

"We're not trying to upset you even more. But if you had told us, maybe we could have helped," Crystal said, this time in a softer voice.

"I don't think there's anything you could have done." Unless they were willing to let me come live with them, there's nothing they could have done.

"You got to tell somebody," Dena said.

"Who? My own mom acts like she doesn't believe me. She has to know I'm telling the truth."

"She knows. She's just in denial," Dena responded.

"I hate her. I hate her as much as I hate Calvin."

"You don't mean that," Crystal said. "You're just upset right now. Give it time to cool down. Your mom will realize you're telling the truth and then she'll kick Calvin out on his behind."

"I don't think so. She's really holding on to the fact that I just said it to break them two up." The pounding in my head increased.

I looked in the direction of the door after I heard a knock. "Open up. We need to talk," Calvin's voice rang from the other side of the door.

I hurried up and got off the phone. "I'll talk to y'all later. I got to take care of something."

Calvin knocked again. I didn't respond. I just sat on my bed with my legs crossed. As usual, Calvin burst into my room uninvited. He seemed outraged. "You've lost your mind going around saying I'm the father of your bastard child," Calvin said.

"Get out. Get the hell out of my room, Calvin. Mama. Mama!" I yelled.

"Your mom took one of her sleeping pills. She had a headache, so she's out for a few hours." Calvin walked in the room and closer towards my bed.

I jumped out of the bed and clenched my fist. I was prepared to fight him today. "Don't come any closer.

You will not touch me again." Without taking my eyes off Calvin, I pulled out the huge butcher knife from under my pillow and held it up.

Calvin laughed. "Little girl, if I wanted to, I could take that knife away from you and stab you with it. But I wouldn't do that because that would kill your mama. Contrary to what you think, I love that woman in there and wouldn't do anything to hurt her."

"I can't believe you, Calvin. You sleeping with her daughter hurts her. Did you ever think of that all the times you've been coming in here and doing what you've been doing?"

"I've tried to stop, but Sade, I love you too. And I can't. I can't be without you Sade."

I extended the knife out in front of me and waved it back and forth. "You're sick. Stay away from me. Stay away from my baby."

Calvin pulled out some money from his pocket and threw it at me as I watched the bills hit the floor. "You can't keep that baby. Get rid of it. If you have the baby, it's going to cause too many problems."

"I can't. Mama don't believe in abortion."

"She doesn't have to know. That's enough money for an abortion and for you to buy you a new outfit," Calvin said, before turning around and exiting the room.

As much as I was upset with Calvin and didn't want to have anything to do with him, I thought about it. I

could not abort my baby. Calvin stole my innocence from me, but he would never take anything else from me. I would keep the money, but I would not be getting an abortion.

~13~

JOYCE

"This has to be a nightmare." The things that Sade said crept into my dreams. Even with me taking the sleeping pills, I tossed and turned in bed throughout the night.

In fact, it didn't feel like I had slept at all. My head ached and felt like an eighteen-wheeler had run right into it. Calvin's snores filled the room. I removed his arm that had been draped around my body so I could get out of bed. He moaned and then turned over and went back to sleep.

I sat on the edge of the bed and looked at the clock. It was thirty minutes before the alarm went off. Thirty minutes before I was supposed to get up and get ready for my twelve-hour shift at the hospital. I tried to will my body to stand up so I could get my day started, but couldn't move. My mind and body wouldn't cooperate.

I reached over to the nightstand and picked up my cell phone. With all that was going on, there's no way I would be able to function at work today. I needed to

figure out how to deal with the Sade and Calvin situation. I called my immediate supervisor.

"This is Joyce. I'm not feeling well and I won't be in today."

I waited for my supervisor to protest, but she didn't. I got off the phone with her and slowly eased out of bed and dragged myself to the bathroom. I stared at myself in the mirror. My red puffy eyes stared back at me. My hair was a mess and sticking up all over my head, but what got me the most was the fact that I no longer recognized the woman behind the ebony eyes staring back at me.

The small diamond of the engagement ring cast a sparkle as I moved my hand in full view of the mirror. I looked at the ring and then back in the mirror to my lifeless eyes. My emotions were all over the place. I felt torn. I loved my daughter, but I loved Calvin too.

How could Calvin do what Sade accused him of and I never knew? Sade had to be lying. There's no way Calvin would do something like that to my daughter. If he had, I would have known.

"Snap out of it," I said aloud, as I turned the cold water on and splashed my face with it. I picked up the small towel from underneath the bathroom counter and wiped my face.

I decided to go check on Sade so I headed straight to her room when I left the bathroom. My eyes caught a glimpse of a knife Sade held in her hands as she slept. I started to go remove the knife, but didn't. "My baby. What's going on with you that you have to lie on Calvin? What guy are you protecting," I whispered.

I quietly entered her room and sat on the edge of Sade's bed. Sade jumped up with the knife in a tight grip. "It's me baby," I said.

Sade blinked and put the knife down when she recognized me. Her head fell back on her pillow. I laid on the bed beside her and said, "It'll be okay, Sade. We'll get through this, together." I rubbed Sade's head like I used to do when Sade was younger. "We'll figure it all out in the morning."

I drifted off to sleep with my body shielding Sade's. I woke up when I felt Sade shift in the bed. "Good morning, sleepyhead,"

I yawned, sat up in bed, and wiped my sleepy eyes.

"I got to pee," Sade said.

I moved over and watched Sade exit her bedroom. I remained sitting there until Sade returned. Sade sat back on her bed, but curled up on the opposite end from where I sat.

I reached for Sade, but Sade shifted her body further into the corner. I wanted to comfort her in some way and make her feel at ease. My hand landed on her leg. "Baby, we're going to get through this. I promise you."

"Is he gone?" Sade asked.

"Of course he's not gone. This has nothing to do with him." I frowned.

"I still can't believe you." Sade had a look of disgust on her face.

I thought once she realized Calvin and I was still going to get married, she would drop the lies. "Sade, this morning, I'm going to take you to the clinic so we can find out for sure if you're pregnant. If you are, we'll get you on government medical assistance so you can get good prenatal care. I want you and the baby to be healthy."

"Mom, listen to you. You act like, this." Sade rubbed her stomach. "Is normal. Me having a baby by your boyfriend is not normal."

My head was starting to hurt again. "Stop saying that, you hear me. I don't want you to say it to no one else. You hear me?"

Sade rolled her eyes. "Whatever."

Okay. I guess playing nice wasn't going to work, so in a stern voice, I said, "Get your ass up and get dressed. We got a long day ahead of us."

I didn't wait to hear her response. All I knew was she had better be ready when I was ready to roll out or all hell would break loose. I heard Calvin's voice before I made it to the bedroom. I walked through the door and Calvin almost jumped off the edge of the bed as he quickly placed his cell phone on the stand as if he hadn't been on it a few seconds ago.

"I thought you were gone to work," he looked up at me and said.

"I got too many things on my mind to concentrate on work. As soon as Sade gets dressed, I'm taking her to the clinic to be tested. We're going to get to the bottom of this one way or another."

Calvin sat on the bed and watched me get dressed.

Calvin said, "You know she's going to hold on to that lie. Don't let her come between us, baby. You know I love you and her so I don't understand why she's tripping out like this."

I went and sat on the bed beside him. I placed my hand on top of his. "I know baby. She's about to turn sixteen and now she might be pregnant. Her hormones are making her act like this."

I said it more to convince myself than Calvin. That was the only excuse I could come up with to justify why Sade was accusing Calvin of doing such a horrible thing.

~14~

SADE

I wasn't trying to eavesdrop, but my mom was talking loud enough for me to hear her consoling the devil. My mom must have stupid plastered on her forehead. Why couldn't she see what was happening right up under her nose? I knew my mom had caught Calvin having affairs with other women, but none of that made her kick Calvin out of our lives. I thought me coming clean about what Calvin did would open up my mom's eyes. I thought she would get rid of that monster once and for all. No such luck.

I looked at myself in the mirror. I felt like my mom was turning her back on me. I thought mothers were supposed to protect their children. If I couldn't depend on my mother for help, then whom could I depend on? I felt completely helpless.

I didn't know what purpose going to a clinic would serve. My mom worked at a hospital so if I needed any medicine, she should be able to get it for me. I got dressed and waited for my mom in the living room on the couch. I could have gone to her room to let her know I was ready, but the way I felt right now, I didn't ever want to see Calvin's face. The less I saw of him, the better it would be for everyone. Every time I saw Calvin, my head hurt and I'm sure that wasn't good for my baby.

"Are you ready?" my mom walked in, interrupting my thoughts.

I decided to give her the silent treatment, but I did stand up and head towards the front door.

Joyce yelled out, "Baby, we're leaving. We'll be back."

I rolled my eyes and walked out the front door.

An hour later, I sat beside my mom in an uncomfortable plastic chair as she filled out sheet after sheet of paperwork required by the state ran clinic. I glanced around the room. There were other teenagers there in the same predicament as me. Some of their stomachs were so big, that it looked like they would be having their babies at any time.

The realization of me having a baby filled my mind. My whole life was about to change. One change that I hated was the fact that I would now have to switch schools because Booker T. had a school policy about girls getting pregnant. Tears filled my eyes as my young life passed right before me. Dreams of being the next R&B teen sensation dissipated in the air. Going to Booker T. Washington was supposed to help

me get out of the hood, but my situation was bound to keep me there a while longer.

"Sade Washington," a middle-aged woman wearing a beehive hairstyle and purple hospital scrubs called out my name.

"Girl, that's you," my mom said.

I followed my mom and the nurse to a room in the back. The nurse took my vital signs and handed me a plastic container to pee in. About five minutes later, I returned with the plastic container and handed it to the nurse.

We were escorted to a private room. The nurse handed me a white hospital gown. "Put this on. The doctor will be right with you."

My mom took the gown from me and opened it up. "Take off your clothes and put this on."

"Why do I have to get naked?" I asked. I wasn't feeling this doctor's visit.

"In order for the doctor to give you an exam, he's going to have to do some things," she responded.

This was all new to me. Why did I have to get naked to get an exam? All the doctor had to do was put a thermometer in my mouth and place that thing on my chest to see how fast my heart was beating. I didn't need to get naked for that. "I wasn't prepared for this."

"Since you're doing grown woman things, you're going to be treated like one, now take your clothes off and put on that hospital gown now."

I took the gown from her hand, but didn't attempt to change.

My mom must have realized I did not intend to get naked. She changed her tone of voice. This time in a calm voice, she said, "It's routine baby. It may feel a little uncomfortable at first. I'll be right here and you can squeeze my hand if it does. Try to think happy thoughts and the exam will be over before you know it."

"Happy thoughts. What do I have to be happy about?" I blurted.

Seeing that I wasn't going to win this battle, I did as I was told. I turned my back to my mom so she wouldn't see my tears. I grudgingly removed my clothes and placed them on the nearby chair.

"You need to take everything off, baby," my mom said.

I already felt dirty and having to get completely naked made me feel worse. I removed my underwear and put the white gown on. My mom shifted the gown around and tied it up in the front. "Now, go ahead and get on the table."

Nervously, I dangled my legs from the table as we waited on the doctor to come. What seemed to be a lifetime, but was really forty-five minutes later

according to the clock in the corner, an older white man wearing a white lab coat and a nurse walked in.

The man said, "Mrs. and Ms. Washington. How are you? I'm Doctor Mack."

My mom responded, "We're fine, Doctor Mack."

He looked at me and then back at my mom. "Mrs. Washington. Sorry for your wait, but we wanted to get the results back before going further. It's confirmed. Sade is pregnant."

My mom gasped. "How far long?"

"We'll know shortly. I want to give her a thorough exam to make sure everything is okay."

I had been holding my breath it seemed the entire time. I sighed. Hearing the announcement from the doctor made it official. I was pregnant. Regardless of what my mom thought, I knew beyond a shadow of a doubt that Calvin was the daddy. My mom could be in denial all she wanted, but that was the cold-hearted truth.

My mom didn't react to Dr. Mack's announcement. In fact, she was unusually quiet. My eyes grew bigger when I saw the plastic weird-shaped thing the nurse placed on a white towel on the counter.

"Sade, this may feel a little cold and uncomfortable at first, but try to relax. It's not going to take long. So just lay back and think of something pleasant."

Easy for him to say. He wasn't the one getting some foreign object slammed up in him. I couldn't think of one happy thought as I endured the uncomfortable pelvic exam. The exam did, however, end quicker than I expected.

"I want to do an ultrasound to confirm how far along you are," he said.

The nurse brought around a device and placed something that felt like cold gel on my stomach. I looked at the screen and saw something really small inside me. It was the making of a baby. I didn't expect to get emotional, but I did.

After the ultrasound, the doctor and nurse left the room and I got dressed. My mom remained quiet. She sat there as if she was in a daze. I was dealing with the hard cold facts of being pregnant so I didn't say anything either.

Dr. Mack returned with his report. He didn't address me; instead, he spoke to my mom as if I wasn't in the room. I saw him hand her a pamphlet. "Sade's two months pregnant. Because she is underage, we have a program that she will need to attend. You're required to go to the first class with her."

My mom flipped through the brochure. "What time? I work. I won't be able to keep taking off work to bring her here."

"Call the number on the back of the brochure and you probably can work something out. It's a six-week

course and I think it's really important for her to attend."

Dr. Mack swiveled his chair around and looked at me. "You'll learn a lot and it'll help prepare you for the little one you're about to have."

Just a few weeks ago, I was worried about Rodrick, but now I had more serious matters on my mind--like the fact that I'm about to be someone's mom and I wasn't anywhere near ready.

My forehead tensed up as my insides boiled with anger. This was all Calvin's fault. He's ruined my life forever. I hated him. I looked at my mom as she listened to the doctor and a strong emotion of hate rose up within me. At this moment, I hated my mom too for loving the monster.

~15~

JOYCE

I listened at Dr. Mack go over the things that Sade would be required to do now that it had been confirmed that she was pregnant. Two months. Which meant seven months from now, I would be some little child's grandmother.

At thirty-five, I wasn't ready for that role. The doctor's results were totally opposite than what I had expected. I expected the trip to the clinic would prove Sade wasn't pregnant. It would then force Sade to admit that she was making things up. I imagined Sade confessing the lie and saying she only faked the pregnancy to break up Calvin and me.

Reality was far from my fantasy. Sade was indeed pregnant and now if I could get her to tell me who the real baby's daddy was, all would be well in my world. As I drove us home, I asked Sade again about the father.

Sade responded, "It's Calvin. C-a-l-v-i-n."

"I was hoping after going to the doctor, you would stop with this nonsense," I snapped. "Again, who is the daddy, Sade?"

She repeated Calvin. I told her she needed to stop with the games. Sounding frustrated, Sade said, "You're going to believe what you want to believe so what's the point?"

I refused to let up on the topic so I asked her again. Sade continued to ignore me and gazed out the window. Music from K104 blasted through the car as we rode the rest of the way home in silence.

Sade headed straight to her room as soon as we stepped into the apartment. I was mentally exhausted so I went to my bedroom. Calvin looked all cool and calm while sitting on the bed playing a video game. All I could do was shake my head. Here I am dealing with Sade's mess and this grown man was playing a video game.

I threw my purse on the bed and sat down on the edge of the bed. "Well, she's pregnant."

Calvin never stopped playing his game. He asked, "So when are you taking her to get rid of it?"

I looked at Calvin as if he had two heads. "No child of mine will be getting an abortion. We will make do. We'll be some young grandparents."

Calvin threw the game controller down. "I'm not ready to be anybody's grandfather."

Before I could respond, Calvin grabbed his cell phone off the nightstand and his keys. He headed towards the front door and I jumped up right behind him. "Where are you going?" I asked, as we neared the front door.

"Out. Anywhere, but here. Maybe, when I get back, you'll have come to your senses."

"Calvin, I don't know what the problem is. It's not like you'll have to take care of the baby yourself. It'll be Sade and me."

"Don't you get it? Sade is out to get me and it's like you're condoning it by allowing her to have that baby. How would you feel if someone accused you of something and you couldn't do nothing about it?"

I didn't have a response to his question.

Calvin looked down at me. "Exactly. I need to clear my head. Don't wait up." With those last words, Calvin walked out the front door.

The floodgates seemed to open as tears flowed down my face. I plopped down on the couch as I thought about the state of my relationship with Calvin. I couldn't bear to lose Calvin over this. Sade had to confess that she lied and soon or else I might lose him--before we could even make it down the aisle.

"Mom, I'm hungry, but there's nothing in the kitchen to eat," Sade came out of the kitchen and said, breaking me out of my trance.

"We'll order a pizza. I don't feel like going to the store."

"Cool. I'll go meet him out front once I order it."

"Call it in and I'll go get you the money."

"I got it," Sade said.

I didn't bother to ask where she got the money to buy pizza. I had to figure out what to do about Calvin. While Sade ordered the pizza, I called Calvin. Every time I called, Calvin manually sent my call to voicemail. I knew that because the phone rang once and then went to voicemail. If his phone were off, it wouldn't ring. It would just go directly to voice mail.

Frustrated, I sent him a text message. "Please come home. We need to talk about this."

My heart skipped when my phone chirped, alerting me to an incoming text. "I don't feel like talking. See you in the A.M."

Livid, I sent him text after text. I waited for him to respond, but he didn't. The last text I sent should get his attention. It read, "If you don't come back home tonight, you might as well stay where you're at. Your stuff will be waiting for you outside the apartment."

"There. I bet you he will get his behind home now," I said aloud, unaware that Sade had returned with the pizza.

Sade placed the pizza box on the coffee table and then handed me some napkins. "Mom, let him go. He's no good. You can do much better."

"Baby girl, you need to stay out of grown folk's business."

"But he's a jerk. Even if he hadn't been messing with me, I would say he was a jerk."

"You're not going to let up, are you?" I asked.

"I have nothing else to lose, mama. Calvin's stolen my childhood from me."

I didn't believe Sade, but I wouldn't let her lie drive a wedge between us. I looked over at the child I had given birth to, reached over, and hugged her. "Baby girl, we'll get through this together."

~16~
SADE

Some of the tension left my body as my mom held her arms around me. I could stay in my mom's comforting arms forever. The sound of the door opening caused us both to loosen our embrace. We turned to face the door. Calvin waltzed in as if nothing happened.

"Joyce, I'm back. Now what?"

"Tell him, mom. Tell him to get his shit and go."

"Sade, watch your mouth," my mom said.

Calvin snapped. "Little girl, you better watch how you talk to me. Joyce, you better control your child."

My mom didn't tell Calvin off, instead she said, "Calvin, ignore Sade. She's upset. Come with me. We need to talk." She got up from the couch and headed towards their bedroom.

"I'm done talking." Calvin picked up one of the pizza boxes, went to the dining room, and sat down. He ate directly out of the pizza box.

My mom returned and took a seat opposite of him at the table. "I'm glad you came back."

My mouth flew open as I watched my mom suck up to Calvin. She just told me that we were in this together, so why in the hell was she all up in Calvin's face like he hadn't done anything wrong.

In a soft voice, my mom said, "Calvin, if we're going to be a family, you can't keep running off every time something doesn't go your way."

"Look. I've been dealing with your daughter disrespecting me for years, but I won't be dealing with my woman disrespecting me too." Calvin stuffed another slice of pizza in his mouth.

"Baby, I'll never disrespect you. You know that." I watched her ease her hand on top of his.

"I've lost my appetite." I threw the half-eaten pizza on top of the pizza box.

I couldn't stand watching the scene anymore. I grabbed my cell phone and rushed out the front door. I paced back and forth in front of the building, but still couldn't calm down. I decided to walk down the street towards Crystal's house.

Some of the neighborhood boys were hollering at me, but I ignored them. I was not in the mood for their immature antics. "Y'all don't want none of this, trust me," I said as I increased my pace.

It didn't take me long to get to Crystal's house. I knocked on the door because their doorbell didn't work. Crystal's mom answered. "Crystal's in her room. Just go knock."

Since I had been there on numerous occasions, I knew exactly where to go. I knocked on Crystal's bedroom door. "Who is it?" Crystal yelled out.

"It's me."

Crystal quickly opened the door. "Girl, I've been trying to reach you. Come on in." Crystal greeted me with a sisterly hug.

Crystal's bedroom walls were filled with posters of Chris Brown, Usher, and Lil' Wayne. We had similar tastes so it wasn't a surprise that she was one of my best friends.

I plopped down in the chair near Crystal's bed and poured my heart out. I told her everything that just happened; including my trip to the clinic. "I can't stand either one of them. I thought my mom was finally coming around and believing me, but as soon as Calvin came back to the apartment, she was busy kissing his butt. I had to get away so I came straight here."

"That's messed up. I can't believe Ms. Joyce would do that."

"Believe it. No matter how much I insist that he's my baby's daddy, she won't believe me. She keeps saying I'm trying to break them up. At this point, I don't give a damn whether they stay together or not. I just want out of that house," I admitted.

Crystal's eyes exuded sympathy. "I can't believe you never told anybody, Sade."

"I was afraid to at first. He told me he would kill my mama."

"Let's call the police. He shouldn't get away with this."

As much as Calvin had put me through, I hadn't thought about calling the police. "Can you call for me? I don't know what to say."

"Tell them what you told me. Your mom's boyfriend has been having sex with you. They'll send somebody out right away," Crystal responded.

Crystal dialed the emergency number and then handed me the phone. The nine-one-one operator said, "Hello is anyone there?"

I cleared my throat. "Yesss. I wanted to report that my." I hung up the phone before I could finish. I couldn't bring myself to do it.

"Why did you do that?" Crystal asked.

"I can't. If I called the police on Calvin and they found out, my mom would hate me."

"But Sade. He should pay for what he's done to you."

"I know, but there has to be another way."

Crystal pulled my arm. "Look at me. Do it. He shouldn't get away with it."

I thought about it. Crystal seemed so positive and I drew upon her strength. I picked up the phone and dialed the emergency number. This time, however, when the nine-one-one operator answered, I said,

"My mother's boyfriend has been sleeping with me against my will. He's at..." I blurted out the house address.

"How old are you?" the operator asked.

"I'm fifteen. Will be sixteen soon."

"Are you in the house now?" she asked.

"No. I'm at a friend's house."

"Stay there. We'll send someone over."

"No, I can't have you come here. I can meet them in front of my apartment building," I blurted. I didn't want to bring this type of drama to Crystal's door.

"Okay, but we don't want the suspect to do anything to harm you."

"Oh, he won't," I said with confidence. Calvin would never expect me to call the police on him. For the first time, in a long time, I felt like I was in control of my life.

"Come on, let's go," Crystal said.

"You can't go. I don't want to bring you into my mess."

"I'm not going to let you go through this alone. Come on. We need to hurry," she said.

"Please. We're in South Dallas. You know the police response ain't that fast."

Crystal agreed. Fifteen minutes later, we sat on a stump in front of my apartment complex. "Just in case some drama popped off. I got your back," Crystal assured me, as we waited.

"Wonder what's taking them so long?" Crystal said as I got up and started pacing back and forth in front of her.

"I don't know. They should have been here by now."

"Sade, get your behind upstairs, now!" my mom yelled from above our heads.

We both looked up and saw my mom's head outside of the hallway window. Crystal followed me upstairs. The front door was wide open.

Before Crystal could walk in, she was blocked by Calvin. He said, "This is a family matter, so Crystal, Sade will be talking to you later."

I turned around and pled with my eyes for Crystal not to go; but Calvin wasn't having it. He eased Crystal out of the doorway and then slammed it.

My mom paced back and forth. Anger was written all over her face. "What do you think you're doing? Didn't I tell you not to tell anyone else that nonsense?" she yelled.

I faked ignorance. "What are you talking about? I haven't told anyone anything."

"Stop lying," Calvin said. He pushed me on the couch.

"Ouch," I yelled as my leg hit the edge of the couch.

SPARKLE

I listened to Calvin rant about the police and going to jail. Inside I was smiling, but I kept a straight face as I pretended not to know what he was talking about.

~17~

JOYCE

Do you know how close Calvin came to getting arrested because of the lies you told?" I spurted out. "If the officer who called hadn't believed me, I would be trying to come up with bail money because of you."

"But, Mama. I didn't..."

Before I could think, I slapped Sade. Sade's hand flew up to her face. Tears flowed down Sade's face. "How could you?" Sade yelled.

"Baby, I'm sorry." I reached for Sade, but Sade pushed my hand back.

"She's the one who should be sorry," Calvin said as he hovered over the both of us.

"Calvin, I need to talk to Sade alone."

"This is my house too and I'm not going anywhere," he yelled as he stood firm in his position.

I tried to diffuse the situation by remaining calm. "Baby, I'm not asking you to leave the house. Just go to another room while Sade and I talk."

"You better get a handle on her or I will. She's taking this mess too far, Joyce. I can't be living like this. Wondering if the cops are going to come arrest me over some lie your daughter wants to tell them." Calvin continued to shout obscenities as he left the room and went back towards our bedroom.

"See what you've done. You've pissed Calvin off," I said to Sade.

"I can't believe you. It's always about Calvin. Maybe, just maybe, if you paid attention to someone, like your daughter, you would see what was really going on."

I was getting tired of Sade and her accusations. I grabbed her by both of her arms near her shoulder. "Look here, young lady. I've been trying to be lenient with you because I know not having your real dad around has to be hard. Shit, my dad was nowhere around either. So I know. But this attitude of yours is threatening to ruin my life. You need to change it and you better not ever…and I do mean ever…call the police trying to get them in our business again. You hear me?"

Sade didn't open her mouth.

I shook her. "I said, do you hear me?"

In a low voice, Sade responded, "Yes."

Satisfied that I got through to her, I dropped my hands from around Sade's arms. "Good. Now, go clean your face. I'm going to cook us a nice dinner and then later on, we can all sit at the table like one big happy family."

Sade obeyed and left the room. I loved my daughter, but Sade needed to stop with her antics before she broke up our happy home. I refused to let that happen so I planned to do whatever it took to hold on to my family.

Tonight, we're having a family dinner and that's just the way it's going to be. I spent the next two hours cooking. I decided to set the table with some of my best dishes. It had been awhile since we all sat down as a family. Maybe this would ease the tension in the household. We needed more family time.

Once dinner was ready, I had Calvin and Sade both come to the table. The tension around the table was thick. No one said anything. The family time wasn't going as I'd planned. I had to laugh at myself. Too much had been said. Would things ever be the same again? I sure hope so. Sade's baby could bring us closer together. Babies usually had a profound effect on people.

"Sade, we'll need to see about getting you into another school first thing next week, okay," I said, in between bites.

"Whatever," Sade responded.

"Don't talk to your mama like that," Calvin said.

"Baby, it's alright," I said in a calm voice. I was trying to make a conscious effort not to blow up at Sade, even when I didn't like her attitude.

"No, it isn't. She's not going to disrespect you. She might be pregnant, but she's still a child and no fifteen-year-old has a right talking to her mother like that."

I gritted my teeth and plastered on a fake smile. "Baby, she's going through some things. We just have to be more understanding."

"Calvin, what you need to do is kick rocks." Sade spoke up loud and clear.

"Forget this. Handle your daughter or I will." Calvin pushed back from the table and stormed out of the room.

"Baby, you can't be flying off at the mouth with Calvin like that. He is going to be your step daddy and he is the man of the house."

"Screw him. Oh, I forgot. I have already." Sade leaned back in her chair and crossed her arms.

"Young lady, you better watch your mouth. Let this be the last time you disrespect me. You hear me!" I forgot about taking the calm approach. I didn't hold back my anger.

Sade rolled her eyes. I raised my hand to slap Sade again, but caught myself. Instead, I dropped my hands and clenched my fists. "What's happened to us?"

"He happened to us." Sade looked in the direction of the doorway.

"Sade, you need to deal with these feelings you have for Calvin. We can't keep living like this. The three of us need to work together and get past this."

"We will never be one big happy family, so you can give up that dream, mama." Sade stared at me without blinking.

I stared back at her. We stood in a staring match. Sade didn't back down. I was the first to look away. I threw my hands in the air in frustration. Nothing I'd done seemed to work. Sade refused to make peace and Calvin was just as stubborn.

~18~

SADE

I retrieved my diary from under my mattress. Dena called so I talked to her as I wrote in my diary. I stopped writing briefly and said to Dena, "I don't know what she thought a 'family' dinner was supposed to do. Draw us closer? Please. My mom has more issues than I do."

Dena responded, "I wish there was something else we could do. Calvin needs his thing cut off."

I laughed at the thought of that. "That would be poetic justice."

There was a lot of background noise from Dena's end of the phone. "Look, Sade. That's my mom and one of her friends. Let me get off here. If you need me, call me back."

I finished writing my diary entry and then called Crystal to give her the latest update. "I can't believe the cops never showed up."

"Well, a social worker is supposed to stop by," I responded.

"Are you going to tell the social worker what's been going on?" Crystal asked.

I shrugged my shoulders. "I don't know. Do you think they will do anything to Calvin if I do? If my own mom doesn't believe me, do you really think anyone else will?"

Crystal stayed quiet for a few seconds and then responded, "It's worth a shot."

"My mom's living in a fantasy world. I thought once I told her, our lives would be different. I had hoped they would be anyway."

I tried to blink back the tears that threatened to fall from my eyes. Lately, I'd been doing a lot of crying. I'm tired of crying. I'm tired of dealing with my mom not trusting me. And I'm really tired of dealing with Calvin.

The sound of the call waiting beeping brought me out of my self-pity party. "Crystal, let me get this call. I'll talk to you later." I clicked over.

"It's about time you answered your phone," Rodrick's voice rang from the other end.

"Rodrick, we have nothing to talk about," I snapped.

"What you saw at the dance is not what you think? I can explain everything," he attempted to assure me.

"Whatever. I have much more important things to deal with. Lose my number please."

"Why? What's going on?" he asked, sounding genuinely concerned.

"None of your business. Have a happy life." I clicked the phone off, hanging up in Rodrick's face.

Rodrick called me again. Each time he called, I hit the ignore button until he finally stopped.

My phone seemed to ring off the hook over the weekend, but I didn't feel like talking to anyone, including my two BFFs, so I avoided talking on the phone and stayed holed up in my room during most of the weekend. I also tried to avoid my mom and Calvin as much as possible. My mom's attempts to hold a conversation with me were unsuccessful. She eventually stopped trying.

I thought about this may well be my last semester at Booker T Washington. It saddened me because it seemed like my dreams were dissolving quickly. I pumped myself up and was determined to enjoy however many days I had left at school. I got dressed in my school uniform and left my room to head to the bus stop.

"Where do you think you're going?" I heard my mom say from behind me as I reached for the front door knob.

"It's Monday and I have school," I responded, without turning around.

"Well, you might as well park it on the couch. When I finish getting dressed, I'm going to sign you up at Fair Park. You know, you won't be able to stay at Booker T being pregnant."

I turned around and faced her. "But mom, nobody has to know. It'll be a few more months before I start showing."

She sighed. "Unfortunately, since we've signed up for the state medical program, your school will be notified, so it's best that we go ahead and get you transferred. I'm really just trying to save you the embarrassment."

This couldn't be happening. My life is going downhill fast. I blurted, "I'd rather not go to school at all."

"Oh, young lady, you're going. You wanted to be grown by gapping your legs open for some guy; it's just a price you have to pay."

I opened my mouth to deny the accusation, but closed it before words could escape. What was the point? She didn't believe me anyway. My whole world was closing in on me. I thought I had at least until the end of the semester. I wasn't even showing so I don't know why I couldn't still go. The idea of having to drop out and go to another school put me in a foul mood.

"Sade, just because you're pregnant doesn't mean your life has to end. I'm going to do whatever I can to help you, but you have to want to help yourself, too."

SPARKLE

My mom talked, but her words bounced off my ears because I tuned her out as I thought about Booker T, my friends, and teachers. I would miss them all. This baby was messing up my life. Maybe, I should do like Calvin suggested and abort the baby and then my world could go back to being like it was. The thought of aborting my baby eased out of my mind just as quickly as it entered. It wasn't my innocent child's fault on how it was conceived. I vowed to love my child more than my mother loved me. I would protect him or her by any means necessary, unlike my mother.

~19~

SADE

Two months later, and four months pregnant.

I took the last two months to get used to going to Fair Park High School. I practically kept to myself. I saw some of the neighborhood girls at the school, but none of them was close to me like my two BFFs. I missed Booker T. I missed my friends.

I stopped thinking about school and thought about why I was here at Crystal's house.

I sat on Crystal's bed as she, Dena, and I talked about our upcoming showcase. "Since you're pregnant and probably shouldn't be doing all those dance moves, we'll let you lead most of the songs," Crystal said.

Feeling as if I was the better singer anyway, I humbly responded, "Okay. Cool."

Finding joy lately was rare for me. The only time I felt happy was when we hung out and got a chance to rehearse for our showcase.

I stood up behind my pretend microphone. I waited for Crystal to hit the record button on her computer to record their session and then I sang a verse of the mid-tempo song.

Crystal sang backup and Dena lip-synched since she couldn't hold a note. When the music went into a lull, Dena took the pretend microphone from me and belted out a few rap verses. Crystal stopped the recording and then played it back.

"We sound good," Crystal said.

"We sure do," I agreed.

"I think we have a good shot at winning this," Dena said as she bounced her head to the beat as Crystal played the song again.

"I heard some record executives are going to be in the audience, so we got to come with our 'A' game," Crystal said.

I was so excited about our showcase that I think I smiled the entire way home. The apartment was dark when I entered. That meant I was home alone and that kept the smile on my face.

I jumped when I heard someone clear their throat. I flipped the light on and saw Calvin. "Calvin, you scared me," I said.

"Your mom's at work, so it's just me and you," he slurred his words.

"Whatever. I'm tired, so can you please move out of the way so I can get to my room?" I asked.

I walked towards the hallway and had to pass Calvin since he was standing near the entryway. He reeked of alcohol. I could smell it on his breath. Calvin's hand reached towards my belly. I jumped back just in time.

"Why Sade? Why?"

"Calvin, you're drunk and you need to chill out man." I tried to remain calm, although I was nervous.

"I told you to get rid of that baby, but now it's too late. Why are you trying to screw up my life?"

"You're a joke. I'll be glad when my mom finally sees you for what you are."

Calvin laughed. "Joyce loves me. She'll never leave me. Haven't you figured that out already?"

I wished he were wrong. My mom's actions validated Calvin's words. Calvin was telling the truth. Sad, but true.

Calvin stepped forward towards me. I dodged him by moving to the right. He lost his step, stumbled, and fell on the floor.

With him being on the floor, it was the perfect opportunity for me to get past him. I rushed passed him to my room, slammed the door and locked it. A month ago, I snuck Crystal's cousin Brandon in the apartment because he knew how to install locks. There were two keys. I had one and Crystal had the other. Keeping my door locked made me feel more

secure and stopped me from worrying as much about Calvin coming into my room uninvited.

My mom was upset when she first learned the door had a lock on it and complained that this was her house and that she should have access to every room, but stopped complaining when I threatened to call the authorities again on Calvin if she didn't allow me to keep the lock on my door.

Calvin beat on the door. "Sade, let me in. I just want to talk to you. I promise not to hurt you. I wouldn't hurt you and our baby."

"At least you're finally admitting it's your baby," I yelled.

"Open up. Come on," Calvin begged.

"No can do. I suggest you leave my door."

"I'm not going to hurt you. I just want to love you. Love you like I used to do," Calvin said.

"Never again." I would do my best to stop him from ever touching me again. I think I would kill him before I let it happen. The day I found out I was pregnant was the day I vowed he would never touch me in that way ever again.

"Come on Sade. You know you like it when I love you."

"Do you want me to call my mama so she can hear how you sound?" I threatened.

"Okay, Sade. You win this round. But don't think you'll keep winning."

I put my ear up to the door and listened as Calvin stumbled away from my room. I left the door locked. My stomach growled. I used some of the money Calvin had given me two months ago for an abortion and bought me a small refrigerator. I kept it filled with snacks and drinks so if I got hungry or thirsty in the middle of the night, I could avoid Calvin and yes, even my mother.

After drinking a bottle of water and eating a snack, I slipped under the covers and drifted off to sleep. I woke up in a cold sweat. I shot straight up in bed. It took a few seconds for it to register to my brain that it was only a nightmare that Calvin had been harassing me, that I was now awake. Awake and alone in my bed.

~20~

JOYCE

After my twelve-hour shift, I decided to go to the grocery store. I would have stopped at the convenience store if I had known the lines would be this long. While I waited on the slow cashier, my thoughts drifted to Sade. I'd been trying to help Sade deal with this situation. I thought going to the classes the social worker recommended would help, but Sade still seemed depressed. No matter how much I've persisted, Sade refused to divulge her baby's daddy name. Sade would repeat the pattern of raising her child without a father, but I decided that I wouldn't kick her out when the baby was born. I would do my best to help Sade raise my grandchild.

This was not in my plans for her. I had hoped Sade would do better in life, but that wasn't Sade's destiny. Having a newborn in our lives would bring a lot of change; changes that I wasn't ready to go through, but at this point, had no choice.

I smiled as I thought about how patient Calvin had been in the situation. Even though Sade was taking us through so many changes, he was hanging in there with me. In fact, he had insisted we marry sooner than later. I agreed with him. If we were married, Sade would have no choice, but to accept Calvin into our lives.

The reason why I was in the grocery store was to purchase a pair of pantyhose. I had the next two days off. Today was a special day for me. No one knew, but Calvin and I had chosen this day to be our wedding day. While Sade's at school, Calvin and I would be going to the courthouse to get married.

After being at the grocery store longer than I had anticipated, I went straight home. I wasn't expecting to come home to an empty apartment. Calvin was nowhere to be found. "Where could he be?" I asked aloud.

Time was of an essence, so I figured Calvin would be back soon. I took a shower to get ready for our big day. After drying off in the bathroom, I rushed to the bedroom hoping to see Calvin. He still hadn't returned. I continued to get dressed. I pulled the dress over my head that I recently bought for this special occasion and then took extra care in applying my make-up and doing my hair. I liked the reflection I saw staring back at me in the mirror.

The off-white, knee-length suit fitted my every curve. I was ready to do this, so where was Calvin? I glanced at the clock. We needed to be registered before ten so we could marry before the judge went to lunch. "Where is he?"

Frustrated, I dialed Calvin's number. It rang several times and then the call would go to voicemail. Two hours later, I was still waiting on Calvin to return. *Something bad must have happened,* I told myself since he wasn't answering the phone or hadn't called. Distraught and resigned to the fact that our wedding wouldn't be happening on this day, I reluctantly undressed.

I swiftly turned around at the sound of Calvin's voice.

"Hey, baby," Calvin said as he waltzed in wearing a pair of jeans and a t-shirt, looking as if he had been playing ball.

My veins almost popped out of my forehead. "Where the hell you've been?"

"Hanging out with the boys."

I looked at the clock and then back at Calvin. "I've been waiting three hours for you. Did you forget? We were supposed to be getting married today."

"Oh, baby. I'm so sorry. With all the drama around here, it slipped my mind. Will you forgive me?" Calvin sat down on the bed next to me and attempted to hug me.

I placed my elbow up, blocking his hug. Calvin ignored my gesture and leaned in anyway. "Come on, Baby. Don't be like that. I'm sorry. We still have time to get to the courthouse and get married before Ms. Thing gets home from school."

I was hurt that he had forgotten. This was supposed to be an important day for us. I should have taken this as a sign not to go through with it, but after looking at the clock and noticing the time, I said, "It'll be one before we get there."

"And. It won't take me, but a minute to change and you. You still look beautiful." Calvin used one of his hands and brushed it across the curls that cascaded down my face.

"I don't know. Maybe this was a sign. Maybe we should wait," I voiced.

Calvin jumped back. "Oh, I see. You're going to use this as an excuse not to marry me. Okay. Well, if you don't want me Joyce, there are other women who do."

"That's not what I'm saying Calvin. I was just looking at the time. We'll have to rush. I don't want our day spoiled."

"You're the one who's spoiling it," Calvin pouted.

"Calvin, you know I love you."

Calvin turned and faced me. "If you love me, show me. Marry me today."

One look into Calvin's puppy dog eyes, I was a goner. I couldn't deny him my hand in marriage. "Yes. I'll do it."

"You sure? No more reservations from you? No more excuses?"

"Calvin, let's get married. Let's tie the knot today as we originally planned," I said.

"Good. Now get your pretty self dressed again so we can get down to the courthouse."

A few hours later, without any fan fare, Calvin and I said, "I do."

The judge pronounced us "Husband and wife."

Calvin kissed me. "I love you," he said, once we stopped kissing.

I beamed with joy and pride as Calvin and I walked out the courthouse hand in hand as husband and wife. I was officially Mrs. Joyce Thomas. I glanced at the gold wedding band Calvin had slipped on my finger and smiled. This was a far cry from the wedding I had back in Shreveport, Louisiana, but I was still happy. I was married to the man I loved.

~*21*~

SADE

Going to school was just something to do. I no longer had the same drive to go like I did when I went to Booker T. I still hoped to get good grades because I wanted to see about getting a scholarship to one of the local colleges. Most of my classes were easy, compared to the classes I used to take, so keeping good grades wasn't a problem.

When I arrived home from school, I was met at the front door by my mom. She seemed excited about something. She had a special glow about her. As I walked through the door, she said, "Sade, go put your books away. There's something I want to share with you."

"I'll be right back," I responded. I rushed and put my stuff away and quickly returned to the living room because I was eager to find out what she needed to tell me.

"Have a seat." She patted the sofa cushion next to her.

I did as I was told. She grabbed my hand. "Baby girl, things are going to change around here for real."

A smile swept across my face. "You finally got rid of Calvin,"

She frowned. "No, baby." She held up her hand.

My eyes zoomed in on the gold wedding band. I stared in disbelief.

My mom went on to say, "Calvin and I got married earlier today. I'm now Mrs. Thomas."

Say what? My mouth dropped open. This felt like a swift kick in the guts. "But...why, mom? You just got engaged."

"Calvin wanted to go ahead and get married. I mean, we've been together for over five years. It's about time, don't you think?"

She didn't really want to know what I really thought because if she did, she wouldn't have married Calvin in the first place. I listened to her go on and on. She sounded like a chatterbox. All I heard out of my mom's mouth was "Calvin. Calvin. Calvin. Calvin wanted this. Calvin wanted that." My head felt like it was going to explode.

She had a disappointed look on her face, but I don't know why she thought I would be happy about her news. She tried to ease my fears by saying, "I promise you things around here are going to change. So, please try to get along with Calvin. Please. For me."

I refused to fake my feelings. "Mama, I will never accept Calvin. Right now, I want to go to my room. I'm feeling sick."

She reached out and rubbed my stomach. "It's not the baby, is it?"

"There's nothing wrong with the baby." I pushed her hand away. I started to say, "It's you. You're the problem," but I didn't. Instead, I got up and went to my room.

As soon as I closed the door, the floodgates of tears flowed down my face. When would my nightmare ever end? My mom married the monster. It felt like the walls were closing in on me. I tried to catch my breath. I kneeled, stumbled over to my bed, and laid down. My attempts on taking a nap failed, so I called up Crystal and Dena to tell them the not so exciting news.

They were just as shocked as I was. I didn't mean to turn my friends against my mother, but from their responses, I could tell they no longer liked my mom. I felt no sympathy for my mom because right now, I couldn't stand her either? The love was quickly fading away and hate was threatening to take its place. I'd tried to keep those negative feelings under lock and key, but this last move of my mom threatened to be the final thread to drive us further apart. I had to do something and do something quick. I couldn't lose my mom completely.

My two BFFs attempted to ease my mind and did their best to get my mind off my current problems. Our conversation shifted and we discussed our upcoming showcase. "We only have a few more days to practice ladies," Crystal reminded us.

"Ugh. Y'all practice without me. I don't feel well." I wasn't faking it either. I really didn't feel well. All of the stress was getting to me. All I felt like doing was curling up in the bed and going to sleep.

"Well, you know your part. Listen to the tape when you're up to it and practice Sade." Crystal said.

"I will," I responded.

"We need you. So don't let us down, okay," Crystal said.

"I won't." I'm not sure why Crystal thought I would let them down, but I wasn't in the mood to pursue the subject further.

I hung up the phone and decided to write a diary entry. Tired and still frustrated, I put up my diary, laid back on my pillows and closed my eyes. I kept having a re-occurring dream. In the dream, Calvin and my mom were getting married. Each time, the preacher would ask, "Does anyone object to this man and woman getting married?" I would object, but Calvin would start laughing and turn to the preacher and say, "She doesn't count. Can we get on with this wedding?" The preacher would continue with the wedding and I was forced to watch the monster marry my mom.

I gave up any hopes of having a peaceful night's rest. I turned on the television with hopes of finding a show to get my mind off my problems. No such luck. All of the shows were corny and boring. I flipped on my lamp and escaped between the pages of the book I had gotten from my mom's bookshelf months ago.

I imagined my life as the main character. Like the character, I wished I had two loving parents. At this point, I wished I had one loving parent. As much as my mom claimed to love me, I no longer believed it. If she loved me, she would believe me when I told her things. She wouldn't have married the man who stole my innocence.

The only person my mom Joyce loved was Calvin. I don't even think my mom loved herself. Even if she didn't believe me about what he did to me, what about the things he'd done to her. If my mom loved herself, she wouldn't have married Calvin because he's cheated on her more times than I care to count. Calvin was a leech and had been leeching off my mom as long as I could remember. My mom was just like some of the women I read about in magazines; desperate with low self-esteem.

When I saw the wedding ring on her finger, the little respect I had for my mom dissolved into thin air. It's hard to respect a woman who continued to

disregard her child's feelings.   My mom did the ultimate no-no. She put a man before her child.

I would never be as stupid as she was. I would never love a man more than I loved myself. I would never be like my mom.

~22~

JOYCE

At first, I thought after getting married, that life in the Thomas household would get better, but instead it got worse. Ever since I delivered the news of our nuptials to Sade, Sade has had an attitude with me. Maybe we should have checked Sade out of school so she could be there for the event. Maybe she was feeling left out. Maybe that was the problem. Then again, with Sade it's hard to tell. She's been so moody since she's gotten pregnant.

"Why are you worried about her? She'll come around," Calvin said as he wrapped his arm around me while we snuggled in the bed.

"But, that's my baby. I hate to see her so upset," I responded.

"She's almost sixteen years old. You baby that girl too much. She has to grow up sometime. Look at her. She's about to have a baby."

"Don't remind me. I wish she would tell me who the real daddy of her baby is so I could at least talk to

his parents. We will need some help and we will be putting him on child support."

"Give it up, Joyce. If she doesn't want to reveal it, let it be."

"If she were your daughter, you wouldn't be saying that." My body stiffened. I didn't feel like cuddling anymore.

"Sade's like a daughter to me so I care."

I turned around and leaned on my elbow, coming face to face with Calvin. "Well, start acting like it. The tension between you two when you're in the same room is so thick."

"I've tried to reach out to her. That's your daughter. I've done the best I can to show her how much I care," Calvin stated. His eyes shifted.

"Try harder."

Calvin pulled me close to him. "Anything for you, but baby."

"What?" I asked.

"I still don't see why you didn't let her get an abortion."

"I've told you, I don't believe in abortion and that's that."

"Whatever. Well, stop with the complaints. Realize you and her will be raising the child without the father in the picture."

"It still doesn't make it right."

"I know a way to help you forget everything," Calvin whispered, as he kissed me.

Less than an hour later, I had showered and gotten dressed for work. Before leaving, I wrote Sade a short note and slipped it under her door. I didn't like Sade keeping her bedroom door locked. She should have at least given me a key just in case she couldn't get out of bed and needed my help. Sade claimed she only had one key, but I'm sure she was lying. I let the issue slide. There was already enough tension between the two of us so arguing about a key wasn't that important.

Calvin's snores could be heard all the way down the hallway. I wished I had the luxury of staying at home and sleeping, but I didn't. My family was quickly expanding and I needed all the hours I could get to help keep a roof over our heads. Calvin was getting too old to hustle. He needed to be more responsible. Calvin wanted to be the head of the household so he needed to get his act together because he had a wife, daughter and soon to be grandbaby to think about. I made a mental note to talk to him about getting a real job later. Right now, I needed to leave so I wouldn't be late for work.

After returning home from a twelve-hour shift, I didn't expect to come back to the sounds of Calvin and Sade arguing. Their voices were so loud, I heard them all of the way out in the hallway.

I fumbled for my keys in my purse and burst through the door, "What the hell is going on here?"

Both got quiet. Sade looked at me and then back at Calvin. "Ask him."

Sade crossed her arms and stared at Calvin. Calvin said, "I don't have time for this. Get your daughter under control or else."

"Tell her, Calvin. Tell mama why we were arguing?" Sade insisted.

"Drop it. I'm getting out of here." Calvin turned and walked away.

Sade rushed and stood in front of Calvin to block him. "Not so fast."

I looked at Calvin and asked, "Calvin, what is Sade talking about?"

Calvin, frustrated, raised and dropped his hand. "I asked her to tell me who the father of her baby is. I was trying to get the information for you, but she got a little hostile."

"That's a bald-faced lie. You wanted me to lie about who the father is. You know good and well, that you," Sade stared at Calvin with venom in her eyes, "Are the father of my baby." Sade rubbed her stomach.

"Little girl, I'm tired of you lying on me." Calvin raised his hand to hit Sade, but I ran in between them and blocked it.

"Calvin, I don't know what's gotten into you, but don't you ever try to hit Sade again. Sade, go to your room. Calvin and I need to talk."

Sade rolled her eyes. "It's about time." Sade stormed out of the living room and back towards her room.

I was pissed. "Calvin, I've never seen you this upset with Sade before. I know we talked about the paternity, but you didn't have to take it this far."

Calvin reached for me. I jerked my body away. "No. That's my little girl there and I know she's now your stepdaughter, but please. You better not ever raise your hand to hit her again."

I stood there for a few seconds. I didn't know what else to do so I walked away. I left Calvin alone in the living room to go get my head together. I went straight to the kitchen cabinet, retrieved a bottle of Crown Royal, and poured myself a drink. I drank it straight. If this didn't clear my head, I didn't know what would.

"Lord, what am I going to do?" I said aloud as I leaned my head back and closed my eyes.

"Don't be calling on the Lord now," I heard Sade say from the kitchen doorway.

"Sade, I'm not in the mood. I suggest you go back to your room or somewhere," I responded, without opening up my eyes.

Sade laughed. "As usual, you're taking Calvin's side, so whatever."

Sade stormed out. I was so upset at Sade right now that I threw the glass at the wall and it fell to the floor and shattered into many pieces. The broken glass reminded me of my life-everything around me was falling apart.

~23~

SADE

I refused to let Joyce and Calvin get under my skin. I avoided them both as much as I could for the remainder of the week. I needed to concentrate on the showcase. Today was the day. I reapplied my make-up to make sure I was on point because we had to look good as well as sound good.

I turned sideways in the mirror and ran my hand across my top. I squinted. I could see my baby bump. I hoped others wouldn't be able to tell too much. My phone beeped. It was a text from Crystal alerting me they were waiting for me outside. I left the bathroom and grabbed my backpack out of my room.

"Where do you think you're going?" Calvin asked, while blocking me in the hallway.

"To mind my own business," I responded.

"Joyce didn't tell me you were to go anywhere."

"My mom's not here so I'm going to hang with my friends."

"I don't think so." Calvin extended his arms so that his whole body blocked the hallway.

I pulled out my cell phone and hit one of the buttons. "Let's see what my mama has to say about you trying to hold me hostage."

Calvin dropped his arms and moved to the side. I hit the end button on the phone and smiled. "Just what I thought. I'll be back when I get back." I pushed passed him and walked out of the apartment.

I slipped in the back seat of Jada's car next to Dena. "Sorry, y'all," I said.

"What took you so long?" Crystal asked, from the front seat.

"Calvin tried to tell me I couldn't go anywhere."

"I can't stand him," Dena responded.

"Who are y'all talking about?" Jada asked.

Crystal said, "Sade's step daddy."

"I didn't know your mama was married," Jada said as she looked at me in the rearview mirror.

I was glad to know Crystal wasn't gossiping behind my back to Jada. The thought of Calvin caused a feeling of disgust to sweep through my body. "She just married the punk. They are still honeymooning."

"I'm glad my mom didn't marry the jerk she was dating," Jada said. "Only thing he did was get drunk and beat on my mama."

"Really. Did he ever beat you?" I asked, out of curiosity.

"Hell no. My brother, Scank, would have beaten him down. My mama used to beg Scank not to whoop up on him after he would beat her."

"Times like these is when I wish I had a brother." I stared out of the window.

"What's up? He ain't hitting you or your mama is he?" Jada asked.

I wasn't in the mood to discuss Calvin with Jada so I responded, "No." I wasn't lying. Calvin wasn't hitting on me, but the pain he caused ran much deeper. "Enough about Calvin. I need to concentrate on making sure I don't forget the words to the song."

Crystal turned around in her seat and looked at me. "Girl, you better not. You got the lead."

I chuckled. "I'm just kidding."

Dena retrieved a CD out of her purse and handed it to Crystal. "Put that on. Let's go over it one more time."

Crystal placed the CD in the player and adjusted the sound. They sang over their song until Jada pulled up into the club's parking lot.

"I'm going to be your manager. Every group needs a manager," Jada said.

Dena laughed. "Girl, you always got a hustle."

"So what do y'all say? When y'all win, you know representatives are going to be hounding you." Jada had a serious look on her face.

Crystal said, "Whatever. We need to win first."

I reapplied some lip-gloss to my lips. "Sure, Jada."
I only appeased Jada since she was our ride.

Jada responded, "Then it's official. I'm your
manager. Well, come on girls. You have a showcase
to win."

Dena said, "Oh no, what did we get ourselves
into?"

Crystal and I laughed.

"I wasn't expecting all of these people. I'm
nervous," I confessed, as we walked in and saw the
other contestants and observers.

"Just pretend like you're in Crystal's room
rehearsing," Jada said.

"Yeah right." I placed my backpack on the floor in
front of me as we stood in the long registration line.

Jada said, "Why don't y'all go find a seat. Dena and
I will take care of registration."

Crystal and I didn't object.

"Let's sit over here." Crystal pointed to a table with
four chairs.

My hand flew to my stomach. I felt the baby kick.
"Please, Lord, please just let me get through this
showcase."

I had to give it to her; Jada was taking her role as
our manager seriously. She made sure we were one of
the top ten performers. Jada barked out orders. "This
is it, ladies. Do your thing! I'll be right over there, so
if you get nervous just look at me."

"I better not," Crystal said.

I said a quick prayer and as the music keyed up, Dena, Crystal, and I walked out on stage.

Sweat formed on my forehead. I hoped it wouldn't run into my eyes or ruin my makeup. The lights were bright, so I could barely see who was in the audience as I stepped behind the microphone.

With my hands slightly shaking, I picked up the microphone and belted out the first stanza. Once I started singing, I forgot all about being nervous. We had all been waiting for this moment. I gave it all I had. Crystal was on point with her background singing and when it was time for Dena to say her rap, she flowed flawlessly.

The crowd seemed to be all up in our performance, and that included some of the other contestants. I walked off that stage with confidence. Even if we didn't win, we were sure to capture some of the A&R representatives' attention that was seated in the audience.

Feeling a little giddy, we went and sat at the table with Jada. "You girls nailed it," Jada assured us.

~24~

SADE

We were on edge as we watched the rest of the performances. We had some stiff competition. Dallas was obviously filled with some very talented people. As I watched some stellar performances, I prayed we would at least rank in the top three.

Four hours later, the judges announced the winners. "Third place goes to Mercedez," the announcer said.

We squeezed each other's hands as the announcer called out the second place winner. "Jon Boy, come on man. You're the second place winner."

"For the grand prize, ten thousand dollars, and a chance to work with one of the hottest producers in the area, the winner is."

Someone walked up to the announcer and whispered in his ear. "Well, ladies and gentleman. I've been informed that we not only have one winner today, but two so the Grand Prize winners will split the ten thousand dollars and both get a chance to work with one of the hottest producers in Dallas. The winners of the Grand Showcase are Black Mafia and one of the hottest girl groups since Destiny's Child."

"Please, please, let it be us," I said. I clenched my eyes shut.

The announcer said, "Adore, come to the stage. You're the other winner of the Grand Showcase."

We were so excited. We couldn't help ourselves. When we heard our names, we all jumped up and down. "We won. We won," we yelled out and hugged each other before making our way to the stage.

The announcer handed the trophy and certificate in our direction. I held the trophy while Dena held the certificate. Crystal acted as our spokesperson. "We would like to thank the judges for believing in us. We can't wait to get in the studio."

After taking photos and finding out more details about our winnings, we piled up in Jada's car. I was elated. One of my dreams was coming true. I was already writing lyrics in my head. I said, "This is it girls. We did it. When I get home, I'm going straight to my room and start working on some songs."

Dena said, "Once you do, call me and I can be working on some raps."

Jada said, "And I'll be trying to figure out how much you girls are going to pay me."

Crystal said, "Excuse me."

"As your manager, I should be paid a salary."

Dena cleared her throat. "Well, according to my research, a manager gets ten or fifteen percent, so unless you get us some more gigs, you don't get paid."

"But..." Jada stuttered.

"Take us to cash our check and then we might give you a little something for taking us to the showcase," Crystal said.

I added, "But it won't be ten percent."

"It sure won't," Dena agreed.

Jada said, "The banks are closed, so I'll have to take y'all Monday."

"Who's going to keep the check?" I asked.

"I'll keep it. No one goes through my stuff," Crystal said.

I looked at Dena. "Dena, I don't have a problem with it, if you don't."

"Sure. But make sure you put it in a safe place."

Jada dropped me off at the apartment. I said my goodbyes and floated out of the car. The smile plastered on my face reflected what I was feeling inside-pure joy. I reached the front door and fumbled for my keys. Even the sight of Calvin and my mom cuddled up on the couch couldn't spoil my mood.

"Hi, mom," I said, when I entered the apartment.

"Hey, baby," she responded.

"Is that all you see?" Calvin asked.

I ignored him. "Mama, I want to tell you something. Can you meet me in my room?"

She looked at Calvin before responding, "Whatever you have to say, you can say in front of Calvin."

"Fine. Me and my friends won a showcase today."

"Really. Well, that's good baby. You do have a beautiful voice." She eased out of Calvin's arms.

"We're going in the studio too to record a CD. Can you believe it?" I couldn't hide my excitement.

My mom's eyes lit up. "Really. Oh my goodness, my baby's going to be a singer." She got off the couch and hugged me. "I'm so happy for you, baby."

Calvin cleared his throat. I guess he couldn't stand my mom giving me attention. "Don't mean to spoil everything, but do they know you're pregnant. How are you going to go to school, record a CD, and have a baby? That's ridiculous. You need to give up on that dream of being a singer. Just concentrate on having that baby and getting your education."

I rolled my eyes. Calvin could take his comments and shove them down his throat. I pretended like he wasn't there. As Evelyn from Basketballs Wives would say, Calvin was a "non-factor" so he might as well get used to it.

I looked down at Calvin as I walked past the sofa and into my room. I threw the backpack on the side of the bed, retrieved my diary from up under my bed and plopped down on top of the covers. I went

immediately to the page where I had written a few lyrics.

I retrieved a notebook out of my backpack and wrote the lyrics out of my diary into it. I hummed along as I wrote them down.

I was still writing lyrics two hours later when my mom asked from the doorway, "Dear, are you hungry?"

Food was the last thing on my mind, but I needed to eat something because of the baby.. "I'll be there in a minute."

I wrote one last stanza, placed my diary and notebook under my pillow, and went to the kitchen to fix me a plate. I loved pasta and was glad to see my mom cooked spaghetti. I piled my plate full with spaghetti and sauce and took a seat at the kitchen table.

Calvin walked in the kitchen and took a seat right across from me. "I meant to tell you earlier that the outfit looked nice on you."

I didn't look up from my plate. I continued to eat and didn't say a word.

"Sade, I just complimented you. Aren't you going to say anything?" he asked.

"I thought you were talking to my mama."

Calvin leaned across the table. "You know you're sexy when you're mad."

I threw the fork on the plate. I was quickly losing my appetite. I pushed back from the table, threw my uneaten spaghetti in the trash and washed my plate.

I turned around and came face to face with Calvin. I could smell the liquor on his breath. He said, "I've been missing you."

"Calvin, please don't go there."

He wrapped his arm around my waist. "You're mine. You'll always be mine."

I struggled to get away from him, but was unsuccessful. "Mama!" I yelled out several times.

"She took a sleeping pill. She won't hear you." He kissed me as I wiggled my body and attempted to get out of his embrace.

I was no match for the drunken Calvin. *Not again,* I thought as I closed my eyes and went to a faraway place.

~25~

JOYCE

The alarm clock buzzed, waking me out of my sound sleep. I reached over and hit the off button. The night before I took a sleeping pill and was able to sleep through the night. I was off today, but forgot to turn the alarm off.

Since I was unable to fall back to sleep, I decided to get up and cook us all a big breakfast. I was at the stove stirring grits when I felt Calvin's arms wrap around my waist. It caught me a little off guard so I jumped.

Calvin kissed the nape of my neck. "You left the bed without giving me my morning kiss."

"You were sleeping so soundly, didn't want to disturb you," I responded, in between giggles as he tickled my neck.

"Well, I'm up now, so what's up?" he said.

"Baby, Sade might walk in. We can take this to the bedroom after breakfast."

"I want you now," he insisted.

I turned around to face him. "Give me thirty minutes, and then I'm all yours."

"Spoil sport," he playfully responded.

"Love you, too." I went back to cooking breakfast.

Ten minutes later, I knocked on Sade's door. "Breakfast's ready. I really would like for you to come sit at the table, dear."

Sade responded from the other end. "I don't feel like it."

"What's wrong? Is it the baby?" I asked.

"Just tired, mom. I'll eat me something later."

I was still determined to bring my family together so I refused to let up. "You need to eat something. Come on, Sade."

"Fine. I'll be out in a minute."

"Hurry up. Don't want your food to get cold," I said, before walking away.

Calvin and I were seated at the table eating our food and joking about stuff. I looked up when I heard Sade enter the kitchen. Her hair was all over her head and she was wearing a robe. She dragged her feet as she made her way towards the stove.

"Well, hello," Calvin said.

Sade didn't say anything.

"Baby girl, it's too early in the morning to have an attitude," I said, before Calvin could say anything else.

Sade turned around, rolled her eyes and responded, "Good morning."

I hated the tension between Calvin and Sade. Things were getting worse and worse as the days went by. Sade fixed her plate and then sat at the table next to me. Sade ate her food, but barely looked up.

"I'm so proud of you, baby," I said, trying to make Sade talk.

"Uh huh," was all Sade said.

"So how much money did y'all win?" Calvin asked. "You know we got some bills around here that we could really use help on."

I interrupted him. "Calvin, let her be. It's obvious she doesn't want to talk to us."

Sade looked up for the first time and in my direction. "Thanks mom."

"Well, I'm just saying. We got bills. She lives here. If she got some money, she should help out."

Sade said, "Like you help out around here. Ha. What a joke?"

Calvin said, "You see how she talked to me. You better get your daughter Joyce. I told you I'm not going to be dealing with blatant disrespect in my house."

Sade pushed her plate away. "I told you I wasn't hungry. And you wonder why." Sade looked directly at Calvin. If looks could kill, Calvin would have been dead from the sharp daggers Sade threw looking his way.

I attempted to diffuse the situation. "Sade, you have to eat something. If not for you, for the baby." I pushed the plate back in front of Sade. "Just eat the grits, if nothing else. Please."

Sade picked up her spoon. "Fine." Sade rolled her eyes at Calvin and then started eating her grits.

"Enough is enough." I was livid. I looked at Calvin and then at Sade. "This is my house. If I can't have peace here, where else can I have it?"

"Now you see how I feel," Sade blurted out.

"Young lady, I've been letting you slide with your smart comments due to your condition, but you will not disrespect me in my own house," I said.

Calvin's face went from a frown to a smile.

Both of them had pissed me off so at this point I didn't care about nobody's feelings, but my own. I turned and faced Calvin. "And you will make more of an effort to be nice to Sade. She's a teenager, not a grown woman, so don't expect her to pay any bills around here. In fact, since we're talking about bills, I think you should find yourself a regular j-o-b and contribute to this household more on a regular basis. I'm tired of bearing the bulk of the responsibility."

Calvin's smile turned into a frown. "Wait a minute Joyce. You have no business talking to me like that."

I stood up and threw down my napkin. "This is my place and I will talk any way I please. Until you start paying more bills around here, you can shut your trap."

Calvin clinched the fork in his hand. His forehead crinkled. "Joyce, I'm warning you."

"Please. I'm going back to bed." I eased away from the table.

As I was passing Calvin, he grabbed my arm. Too tight at that. "Don't you ever raise your voice and talk to me like that again. You hear me?"

He caught me off guard. Words eluded me. His fingernails dug into my arm. I tried to jerk my arm away, but Calvin had a firm tight grip and squeezed my arm tighter. Before I could react to the pain of his fingernails, Calvin slapped my head with his hand.

"Oh my God," I yelled out in pain and in shock.

At this point, I'm able to free myself from his grip. I cursed him.

Calvin tried to reach out to console me. He said, "Baby, I'm sorry. I didn't mean to hit you. You made me do it."

"Leave me alone!" I ran down the hallway to our bedroom. I slammed the door and locked the door from the inside.

My back was on the door as Calvin banged on the door yelling out apologies. "Joyce, I'm sorry. It's the stress. It's getting to me. Please, baby, open up."

"Calvin, go. I don't want to see you right now."

My body slid down the door onto the floor as I thought about what had just transpired. I never thought Calvin would raise his hand to hit me. "Ouch," I said aloud as my hand touched the bruised spot on my face.

Calvin kept yelling from the other end of the door, but I refused to open it. I remained sitting on the floor in the same position until I heard the front door slam shut. I unlocked the bedroom door and to my surprise, Sade was standing right on the other side.

"My baby, I'm so sorry you had to see that." I immediately embraced Sade.

"Mama, are you okay?" Sade asked.

"I'm fine now, honey." I pulled away and looked at Sade. "I'm fine. Just fine." I repeated myself, but didn't really mean it.

~26~

SADE

I went back to my room after my mom assured me she was okay. I laid across the bed and thought about what had happened. As much as I was mad at my mom for believing Calvin over me, I couldn't bring myself to hate her. When Calvin attacked my mom, I felt helpless. Instead of helping her, my body remained glued to the chair. This was the first time I'd seen Calvin physically attack my mom. I now wondered if this was a first time thing or did it happen before and I just didn't know. Like my mom didn't know Calvin was doing those things to me.

Soon as I heard Calvin leave, I ran to their bedroom. It broke my heart to hear my mom cry from the other side of her bedroom door. Soon as my mom opened the door and pulled me into her arms, I forgot about being angry with her. I held on to her so she would know that she wasn't alone. Although my mom hadn't been there for me, I didn't have the heart to abandon her at this time.

Since my door wasn't completely closed, my ears went on alert when I heard the front door open. I rushed to my door, but didn't close it. I peeped through the crack. Calvin eased by my door and headed to their bedroom. Their door wasn't locked because Calvin turned the knob and walked right on in.

A few minutes later, I heard Calvin and my mom shouting at each other. They were so loud; I didn't have to stand by the door. I sat in my bed and heard their verbal exchange. After arguing for what seemed like half an hour, I expected to hear Calvin leaving again, but instead, I heard them making sex noises.

"How could she take him back after that?" I couldn't wrap my head around what I was hearing.

I hated Calvin more and more with each passing day. I couldn't figure out what kind of hold Calvin had over my mom. It irked me so much I wanted to scream, but screaming wouldn't do any good, so I didn't.

I sat there and dealt with conflicting emotions about my mom. A part of me hated her for allowing Calvin to hurt her and me, but Joyce was my mother, so I still had a soft spot in my heart for her. It would make life so much easier if I could outright hate my mom.

I dialed Crystal's number and told her about Calvin hitting my mom. "Can't she see Calvin's a menace and needs to be put out of our lives?"

"She's in love," Crystal said, dragging out the word love.

"If love make you do stupid stuff like that, I don't ever and I mean ever want to be in love," I responded.

Crystal smacked gum in my ear as she talked. "I know that's your mom and things, but somebody need to tell her a thing or two. My mama said, if it was her, she would have been kicked his sorry behind out of her house."

I could hear my drunken mother slurring those words too. "Well, maybe she could talk to her because he's cheated on her, he's now beating her. I don't know what else has to happen to get her to get Calvin out of our lives."

"I'll ask her. Do you want me to share with my mom about what Calvin used to do to you? My mom did ask me if I knew who your baby daddy was."

"Your mom needs to mind her own business," I said to myself. To Crystal, I said, "I don't care. I ain't trying to protect Calvin's reputation."

"I'll tell her and we'll see what happens."

"I doubt if it works, but anything is worth the try." I laid on my back and rubbed my stomach.

"Tomorrow after school, Jada's going to take us to deposit our check," Crystal said.

"With all of the drama going on around here, I haven't even been able to think about our winning and what it means," I admitted.

"Cheer up. If this works out, you can move out of your mama's house and never have to see Calvin again."

I sat up in bed. "It happened again."

"What happened?" Crystal asked.

"It," I repeated.

"Nooo. Say it ain't so. I thought you kept your door locked now," Crystal said.

"I do, but he cornered me in the kitchen yesterday. I tried to fight him off, but he's stronger than me and the next thing I know, he's all over me..." my voice trailed off. I wiped the tears that fell from my eyes and cleared my throat.

Crystal said, "Sade, you got to get out of there. He can't keep doing this to you. It's just not right."

"What else can I do? I called the police, but that didn't work out. They sent out a social worker one time and I guess her report came back good because I haven't seen another social worker."

"If your mom isn't going to do anything about Calvin, Sade you have to do something."

"But what?" I really wanted to know. I was tired of playing the victim.

Crystal responded, "I'm going to tell my mama, now."

Before I could protest and stop Crystal, Crystal had hung up the phone.

A few minutes later, Crystal called me back. "My mom said she's coming over there right now."

"Is she drunk?" I asked.

"Uh, no and even if she is, she knows how to handle her liquor."

"Yeah, right," I responded.

"So open the door. I'm coming with her. We'll be there in a few minutes."

"Crystal, maybe you should stay at home. There's no telling how my mom's going to react."

"I know. That's why I'm coming. I wouldn't miss this for the world," Crystal responded.

~27~

JOYCE

B aby, I got an errand to run and it won't take long," Calvin said as he slipped on his pants.

"But, you just got back." I pulled the covers over my body.

Calvin leaned over and kissed me on the lips. "I'm so glad you forgive me. I had to come home to make sure things were okay with you. I can't stand for you to be mad with me."

"Just make sure you never do what you did to me again."

"I promise. It's Sade. She just gets under my skin sometimes and I took out my frustrations on you, baby. I promise to never do it again."

I watched Calvin leave, but since I wasn't sleepy, I decided to go to the bathroom to wash up and get dressed.

As I was leaving the bathroom, I heard a knock at the front door. "Sade, can you get the door?" I yelled.

Sade didn't respond. Not in the mood to deal with one of my nosy neighbors, I cursed under my breath. I didn't bother to ask who was on the other end. I yanked the door open.

Crystal and Maddie, Crystal's mother, were standing right in front of the door.

"Maddie, how are you? What are you doing here?" I asked, surprised to see them both standing there.

"Came to check on you," Maddie responded. She stood a few inches taller than me and at least twenty pounds lighter.

"Come on in." I moved to the side and allowed Maddie and Crystal to walk in. I addressed Crystal, "Sade's in her room. You're welcome to go on back."

"Yes ma'am," Crystal responded and left Maddie and me alone.

"Girl, now why did I have to hear through the grapevine that you got married?" Maddie asked, as she plopped down on the couch.

I took a seat on the opposite end of the couch. "Well, we just recently did it and I wanted to get used to being Mrs. Thomas first." I extended my hand to show Maddie my ring.

Maddie eased over so she could get a closer look. "Joyce, you and I are friends right?"

What I did in my personal life was my own business, so I didn't feel like I owed her or anyone else an explanation. I squinted my eyes. "Yeah, of course."

"I found out some things that I think you should know. Please don't get upset with me. I'm only here to help."

I crossed my arms and leaned back in my seat. "Just spit it out."

"Is Calvin sleeping with Sade?" Maddie asked without flinching.

I immediately uncrossed my arms. "Hold up. How are you going to come up in my place and ask me a question like that?"

Maddie responded, "If he is, you need to get that pervert out of your house. Crystal tells me that he's the father of Sade's baby."

"Do you realize how sick that sounds?" I asked.

"Yes, but do you?" Maddie looked me in the eyes.

"Calvin is not a child molester and I don't know why Sade is going around accusing him of something he hasn't done. She's been sleeping with some boy and won't tell us who it is."

"Stop trying to protect that bastard." Maddie gritted her teeth.

"He's not guilty of anything. He's done nothing but love that girl."

Maddie shook her head. "Joyce, do you hear yourself? You're taking up for a man who has harmed your daughter in a way that can never be revoked."

If this was all Maddie had to say, she could keep her comments to herself. I didn't need her or anyone else telling me how to run my household. This was our problem and we would deal with it. She needed to be concerned about herself, go to AA or something, and deal with her own problems. She's the drunk, not me.

I was pissed. I stood up with hands on my hip. "Maddie, you are my friend, but for you to come to me with this shows me you really aren't."

"Sade is like a daughter to me. Anyone who harms her makes it my business. If you don't get that man out of your house, then I will have no choice, but to call the police."

I pointed toward the door. "Get out!" I yelled. "You will not disrespect my husband."

Maddie shook her head from side to side and got up out of her seat. "I never thought I would see the day that a woman would put a man before her child. You don't give a damn about nobody but yourself. Have you thought about how this has affected Sade? No you haven't."

"I said get out," I repeated. I was seconds away from jumping on Maddie so if she knew like I knew, she better leave before I did.

"Oh, I'm going. You don't have to tell me twice. "With you allowing Calvin to harm Sade, you are just as guilty as he is. I don't want to be in the house with two child molesters."

That was it. That's the final straw. "How dare you call me a child molester?" I yelled, right before throwing a punch Maddie's way.

"What the hell?" Maddie staggered back just in the nick of time.

We swung and hit at each other until we both got tired. When we were through, we both looked a hot mess. I hadn't gotten into an altercation with another woman in years so I was a little rusty, but I bet Maddie would learn to keep her comments to herself from now on. I felt better after getting in a few blows.

Maddie stammered away from me while trying to brush her hair down and fix her clothes. "Crystal!" Maddie yelled. "Come on. We're getting out of this hell hole."

"Mama, I'll walk home later," Crystal walked out and responded.

Her and Sade looked at us, but didn't say a word.

"No daughter of mine will be around a child molester." Maddie grabbed Crystal's arm. "Come on."

Crystal shrugged her shoulders as Sade stood nearby. "I'll call you later," Crystal said to Sade.

Maddie stopped in front of me with a look of disgust on her face. "You." She looked me up and down, with her nose turned up and said, "You disgust me."

"Maddie, I said, get out of my house." Fury seemed to pour through my pores. I was on the edge of pouncing on her again if she didn't leave.

"Gladly," Maddie said as she pushed Crystal out of the door ahead of her.

As soon as they walked out, I walked to the door and slammed it. I caught Sade staring at me. "I should beat your ass for telling my business to that woman."

"Mama, I didn't tell Ms. Maddie anything. Anyway, everything she said is true. Calvin is a child molester and you're letting it go on." Sade leaned on the wall and crossed her arms.

"When Calvin gets home, we're going to get to the bottom of this. I'm tired. I'm sick and tired of all of this." I threw my hands up in the air and stormed past Sade.

~28~

SADE

*C*rystal called me as soon as she got home. "Are you okay?" Crystal asked.

"I guess. My mom's in serious denial. She's pissed at me and your mom."

"She'll get over it. I've never seen my mom this upset. She's forbid me to come back to your house. Says it's not safe with Calvin being there. She doesn't want anything to happen to me."

I was disappointed and a little hurt by Crystal's mom comments. "I understand," I lied. "I'm only here because I have to be. If I had somewhere else to go, I would be gone."

"I wish we had room here. Maybe you could come camp out with me. I'm sure my mom wouldn't mind."

I rubbed my belly. "If it was just me, she probably wouldn't. I doubt if she would welcome me in with my condition."

"Yeah, you're right," Crystal agreed.

"Sade, come here," Joyce yelled from the other side of the bedroom door.

"That's my mom. Let me go see what other kind of drama is about to pop off. I'll call you later."

I eased off the bed and unlocked my door. My mom stood in the hallway. "Come with me to the living room. We're going to have a family meeting."

I threw my head back, rolled my eyes, but obeyed my mom. I followed her into the living room. Calvin was there seated on the couch. My mom sat next to him. I walked around them and took a seat in the chair. In the position I sat, I felt like I was in the hot seat as they both stared back at me.

"Calvin and Sade, I love you both," I said as she looked back and forth between the two of us.

"I love you too, mama," I responded.

Calvin didn't respond at all. He didn't seem too thrilled to be in our family meeting. His cell phone beeped. He picked it up and looked at the screen. "Can we hurry this up? I got money on this game and I need to make sure I'm winning."

My mom placed her hand on his thigh. "This won't take long. Just need you two to be honest with me."

I wanted to laugh. Calvin didn't know the definition of honesty. I held a smirk on my face. "What do you want to know, mama? I'll tell you everything and I do mean everything." I looked at Calvin as I spoke.

Calvin said, "Joyce, I don't have time for Sade's games."

My mom pled, "Wait. Sade, be quiet for a minute and let me handle this."

"Okay." I twisted in my seat, sat back, and crossed my arms.

My mom placed her hand on top of Calvin's. "Baby, you know I love you, so don't get mad at me for asking. I just need to know. I'm not going to love you any less. We're a family and we can get through this together. I just need for you to be honest with me, okay?"

Calvin had a nonchalant attitude. It was written all over his face. "Joyce, I don't have all day. Just ask what you want to ask so I can go watch my game."

"Have you ever touched Sade in an inappropriate manner?"

Calvin pushed her hand away from his. "How you going to ask me something like that?"

"I keep hearing these things."

"Are you going to believe the stuff you hear out in the streets or are you going to believe me, your husband? The man you promised to love, honor and obey!" Calvin yelled.

"Calvin, calm down. I'm just tired. Sade's accusing you of stuff and I just need to hear it from you that you didn't do what she accused you of."

Calvin stood up. "You're both crazy. No wife of mine should be accusing me of doing something sick.

I can't believe you Joyce. I thought what we had was solid, but now I'm not so sure."

Calvin grabbed his keys off the table. "Don't go Calvin, we can talk about this," my mom begged.

"I'm not talking about nothing. I'm out of here. When you feel like apologizing for accusing me of some shit that your daughter made up, then call me." Calvin held the front door opened. "Otherwise, I'll see you, when I see you."

Without saying another word, Calvin walked out and slammed the door.

My mom ran to the front door and opened it. She yelled, "Calvin, come back."

Calvin apparently ignored her because he never came back. She shut the front door and sat back down on the couch. With watery eyes, she looked at me. "See how your lies are breaking up this family?"

My hands flew up in the air. "Oh my God. Mama, you talk about you're tired. I'm tired of explaining myself to you. For once, I want a mom who will have my back and take up for me for a change."

"But, don't you see what these lies are doing to me. I love both of you. I shouldn't have to make a choice of whose side I'm on," she said.

"I'm your daughter. There shouldn't be any choice. You should know that I wouldn't make it up. You should trust me enough to know that, but instead you're so busy following up behind him."

"Sade, you are way out of line now. I hear what you're saying, but none of it makes any sense to me. I would have known if Calvin was doing something to you. You never said anything, so why make it up now?"

Talking to my mom about Calvin was like talking to a brick wall. Everything I said bounced right off her. The pain in my heart pierced right through my soul. I didn't know what else to do or what else to say. I felt hopeless and wondered if my mom and I would ever be able to recover from this breach in our relationship. I eased up out of the chair. "Whatever mom. You're going to believe what you want to believe. You didn't even notice he never really answered your question, now did he? Ask yourself why? Because he's guilty. Guilty. Guilty. Guilty!"

~29~

JOYCE

My head hurt. The stress of Sade's accusations and Calvin's attitude had me on the verge of a nervous breakdown. Sade went to her room and I remained in the living room; trying to make sense out of what had transpired. I dosed off on the couch. When I woke and saw how late it was, I went to my room and called Calvin.

Calvin's phone calls went straight to voice mail. I cursed him out on several messages. I threw the phone on the side of the bed and attempted to get some sleep. I tossed and turned all night, hoping Calvin would return home. Throughout the night, I recalled how Calvin never came out and said, "No, Joyce, I never touched Sade."

Could what Sade had been saying about Calvin all of this time be true? *No, it couldn't be. Calvin loves me. He would never hurt me or hurt my daughter in that way.*

A part of me didn't want to believe the words coming out of my mouth, but my mind and heart refused to believe that of Calvin.

I was in deep thought when Calvin staggered in our room smelling like yesterday's garbage. "Calvin, where were you? I've been worried about you," I said.

"Somewhere where I'm wanted," he responded. He peeled off his clothes.

"I hope you weren't with another woman. If you were, you can leave because I dealt with you cheating before we got married, but adultery is something I will not tolerate," I snapped. I meant it. We could work through anything, but him cheating on me now that I was his wife was out.

"Woman, I was not cheating on you."

"Then what kept you out all night? You're married. You should have been sleeping in your own bed."

"You should have thought about that before you came at me the way you did last night," Calvin snapped.

"I only did what I thought was best. I'm tired of the tension in this house. I'm stressed out at work. I'm stressed out at home. I have no peace."

"That's not my fault. If you stopped trying to please everybody, then you would."

"Calvin, all I wanted to know is why did you storm out and stay gone all night? We're supposed to be able to talk about anything."

"We should, but lately, you've been so busy trying to please that lying daughter of yours, that it's coming

between us. I told you I'm not going to deal with disrespect in my own house."

"I'm only trying to get to the bottom of the situation," I responded.

"You'll get enough of falsely accusing me of stuff." Calvin grabbed a clean towel and stormed out of the room to the bathroom.

"I hate you," I heard Sade yell from out in the hallway.

I jumped out of the bed and headed straight to the hallway. "What's going on here?" I asked.

Calvin stood in front of the bathroom and Sade stood out in the hallway. Sade looked at me. "Ask your husband!" Sade stormed off and went to her room. The next sound I heard was Sade slamming her bedroom door.

"Calvin, what is Sade talking about?" I stood still with my arms folded.

Calvin ignored me. He went into the bathroom and shut the door. *Oh, no, you're not going to ignore me.* I ran to the door and turned the knob. It didn't bulge. I beat on the door. "Calvin, open up and answer me. What was that about?" Calvin wasn't making the situation any better with his funky attitude. Was there some truth in what Sade had been saying? If it was, Calvin would have hell to pay. I was determined to get to the bottom of this situation. I beat on the bathroom door again.

"Joyce, I'm tired. I want to take a shower and get some sleep. Can a man get that when he comes home?"

Since Calvin was being bull-headed and wouldn't open the door, I decided to go talk to Sade. I knocked on her door, but she didn't respond. Surprisingly, when I turned the knob, the door opened. Sade was curled up in the corner of her bed with her pillow staring out into space in the dark room.

I flipped the light on. "Sade, what happened out there?"

Sade looked at me, but didn't move. "The same thing that always happens when he gets me alone."

"Did he touch you?" I asked.

"No, he looked at me funny like he always does," Sade responded.

I laughed. I couldn't believe it. All this drama because he looked at her funny. "Come on, now. You can't be mad at someone for looking at you."

"He has no business looking at me with lust in his eyes."

I had no response. I felt caught in the middle. It was a he said, she said type of situation. I loved them both and if I were to be honest with myself, I didn't know whom to believe.

Sade tilted her head up and said."If you don't get him out of here, I'm leaving. Living on the streets

would be better than living under the same roof as that pervert."

"Stop it. Just stop it. You're not going anywhere. You have a baby to think about too."

Sade laughed. "You don't care about me and you don't care about my baby."

"Sade, I love you. I love you more than anything in the world. Talking to the both of you didn't work, so just give me some time to figure out what needs to be done."

"Whatever," Sade responded.

Dejected, I left the room. It seemed that Sade had lost all faith in me. I tried to look at things from her point of view, but I also had to look at the total picture. Things just weren't adding up and until they did, I had to take my neutral stance. I glanced at my reflection in the mirror. I didn't like what I saw. What stared back at me was a frail woman who had lost control of her life? How could I regain myself? I didn't know how much more of this I could take.

~30~

SADE

I woke up to Calvin and my mom's loud voices. I felt bad leaving my mom alone to deal with Calvin, but I had to get to my bus stop. If I didn't leave now, I would miss my bus. I looked down at my stomach. It seemed to have grown overnight. None of the clothes I put on fit me properly anymore.

I left the apartment without telling my mom I was gone. I wouldn't be missed. I'm sure.

"Hey, girl," Crystal said to Sade as she neared her old bus stop.

I only had a few minutes to talk. I stopped and held a brief conversation with Crystal. "There goes my bus. I'll see you later," I said, right before rushing to catch my school bus.

My eyes watered as I viewed from my bus window Crystal walking on to my old school bus. It was times like these that I missed Booker T. My neighborhood school wasn't bad because I grew up with most of the kids, but it wasn't anything like Booker T.

Instead of being active, I found myself being withdrawn at school. I didn't make much effort to

make any new friends. My only goal was going to class and passing to the next grade. Being at school, took me away from the problems at home. With all that was going on, maybe I should have stayed at home with my mom, today.

"Ouch," a deep male voice said.

I had accidentally run smack into the middle of a tall, mocha colored boy with the deep voice. "I'm so sorry," I said, apologetically.

"I'll forgive you, if you'll give me your number," the stranger responded.

I moved my books. Giving him a good view of my protruding belly. "You might not want that."

The stranger wouldn't give up. "You having a baby shouldn't stop us from being friends now should it?" he asked.

"Of course not," I responded.

"Then, I don't see a problem." He held out his hand. "I'm Brandon Lockett."

"Sade Washington," I responded, shaking his hand.

"What a pretty name? Sade, I'll be seeing you around. Maybe next time you'll slip me that number."

"Why put off later, what you can have now." I wrote my number down and handed it to him. I tried to play it cool, but inside I was excited that the cute guy had asked me for my number.

"I'll be calling you," the guy assured me.

I smiled as I headed to class. My day at school went by without any drama. My body immediately tensed up the moment I stepped foot inside of the apartment. I called out, "Mom, are you here?"

Her car was parked outside, so I knew she wasn't at work. When I didn't get a response, I dropped my backpack by my bedroom door and then headed towards their room. The door was ajar so I peeked in.

The sight of my mom sleeping wasn't abnormal. What was abnormal was her huge puffed up black eye. I covered my mouth as I gasped.

"Sade, is that you?" my mom whispered.

"Yes, mama." I rushed to her bedside.

I reached out to touch her face.

She blocked my hand. She said, "Don't. It hurts."

"Did Calvin do this to you?" I already knew the answer, but wanted her to tell me.

"He was mad. I made him do it. I shouldn't have badgered him about answering my questions."

"Mama, this is not your fault. Calvin needs his ass kicked."

"Watch your mouth," she said as she coughed.

I noticed red marks on her neck. "Did he choke you too? Mama, you need to call the police. This is assault."

Calvin burst in the room. "Little girl, you better stay in a child's place. What goes on with me and your mother is just our business."

He stood near the foot of the bed. A part of me was scared because Calvin had crossed the line with my mom physically so I wasn't sure what he would do to me.

Regardless of being scared, I boldly stood up and said, "You bastard. Keep your hands off my mama."

Calvin twisted his head from one side to the other. He laughed. "Sade, I'm not playing with you. Your mom needs to rest, so I suggest you leave her and me alone right now."

My mom shifted her body in an upright position, grunted and said, "Sade, baby. I'm okay. I just need to get some rest. Go do your homework or something."

"But, mama."

"Sade, I'm okay," my mom yelled.

I didn't want to leave her. As much as she protested, I knew she wasn't okay. She was allowing the monster to get away with something else. When would the abuse ever end? I eased past Calvin as he stood near the end of the bed. He reached out towards me, but I was too fast for him and rushed out the room. He laughed. I didn't.

My phone rang. It was still in my backpack, so I ignored it. Once I was safely sitting on my bed, I took the phone out of it and scrolled through my missed calls phone log. There was a call from Crystal and a text message. I immediately dialed Crystal's number. Before I could say anything, Crystal blurted out,

"We're on our way to swoop you up so we can go cash our check."

"Good, because I need to get out of here before I kill someone."

"Did Calvin try to touch you again?" Crystal asked.

"I'll tell you everything when y'all come pick me up." I hung up and quickly changed out of my school uniform into something else. The loose fitting black pants and top felt more comfortable.

After I dressed, I grabbed my phone and keys and sat outside of the apartment complex to wait on Jada, Crystal, and Dena.

Jada swooped her car out front. "Hi, y'all," I said as I slipped in the back seat.

"What's up?" Dena asked from the other side of the back seat.

I gave them an update on the latest drama in my household.

"Your mom stupid," Jada blurted out.

"Jada, she's still my mom."

"No way would I be letting a man beat up on me," Jada said. "That's all I'm saying."

I'm glad Crystal and Dena hadn't shared what else Calvin had been doing. With her comments, I definitely didn't feel comfortable talking to her about it.

Crystal intervened, "I hate to see your mom go through this too."

"Let's talk about something else. Like when do we get in the studio? Ms. want to be our manager, can you tell us that?" I asked, looking up at Jada's eyes in the rearview mirror.

Jada responded, "Ha. Ha. Yes. We should meet with the producer as soon as next month."

"Next month. Cool. I hope it's on my birthday. That'll be a great birthday present."

"When's your birthday?" Jada asked.

"The sixteenth."

"She'll be sweet sixteen," Dena said.

I looked at Dena. "Ain't nothing sweet about me turning sixteen."

"Awe, it can't be that bad," Jada said.

"Trust me. It is," I responded and then looked out the window.

~31~
JOYCE

The tears flowing down my face stung my swollen eye. I tried to stop crying but couldn't. Calvin just finished making love to me and telling me how sorry he was for hitting me. He put the blame on me. He said it was my fault for pushing him over the edge.

How did my life get to this point? Before marrying Calvin, he had never laid his hands on me. This was the second time he'd attacked me physically. I worked at a hospital so I met battered women all of the time. I could never understand how a woman would allow a man to harm her physically. Did their abuser promise he would never do it again, like Calvin? Was their love so deep that they overlooked the abuser's actions? I didn't understand until now because I now stood in those women's shoes.

Calvin's apologies fell on deaf ears. The first time he apologized, I forgave him, but this time. This time would be different. I had to call into work again. Fortunately, I had some sick time. But still, I was the supervisor. I couldn't keep taking unscheduled time off.

SPARKLE

As soon as Calvin fell asleep, I eased his arm from around my body and got out of the bed. I jumped when I saw how bruised my face looked in the bathroom mirror. My hand automatically went up to my face. I touched the swollen spot around my eye. This was my first time looking into the mirror since Calvin hit me. I had no idea I looked this bad. One of my eyes was so puffy, it looked like it was unattached to my face and if you stuck a pin in it, it would burst.

My entire body hurt. I ran some hot bath water in the tub. I eased my body in the bubbling suds. I "oohed" and "awed" as the warm water soothed my aching body. I leaned my head back on the towel I had folded and draped on the back of the tub. My mind reflected over the last twenty-four to forty-eight hours.

I thought about Sade. Sade tried to help me, but I pushed her away. I could take the abuse. I didn't want Sade getting involved because with tensions flared, I didn't want Calvin to get violent with Sade too. Contrary to what Sade thought, I did love her. I had unconditional love for her. The love I had for Calvin was a different kind of love. I loved them both and that's just the way it was.

I stayed in the tub so long that the water turned cold. I slowly eased out of the tub and dried off my body. I moaned in pain. My face hurt as I brushed my teeth. I fumbled through the medicine cabinet until I

found the pain medicine I was looking for. I dropped two of the pills in my mouth, turned on the faucet, and put water in my hand. I brought the water up to my mouth and swallowed the pills.

As much as it hurt, I blinked my eyes a few times. I looked in the mirror and said, "You got to get it together. If not for you, for your child and your grandchild."

I wiped my face again and then left the bathroom.

"Joyce, baby, where are you?" Calvin yelled from the bedroom.

I was just about to knock on Sade's door when I heard Calvin call out. I dropped my hand before knocking, turned, and walked back to my bedroom. I stood in the doorway. Faked a smile and responded, "Yes, dear. What do you want?"

"Just trying to see where you were. What are you doing?" he asked.

"I took me a bath. Is that okay with you?" I tried to speak in a calm voice. I was irritated with Calvin and myself.

"I was just checking on you," Calvin said as he sat up in bed.

"I would be better if you didn't lay your hands on me," I mumbled.

"Joyce, I told you I was sorry. Stuff happens. You pushed my button and I snapped."

"Well, don't let it happen again."

"I won't. I promise," Calvin assured me once again.

I walked away and went back to Sade's bedroom door. This time I knocked. "Come in," Sade responded.

"I know I've been ghost for the last couple of days. Just wanted to check on you."

"I'm fine," Sade responded.

"I'll be going back to work tomorrow and I'll be on the night shift."

"Thanks for the warning."

"I'm not warning you, just letting you know."

"I'll be sure to keep my door locked," Sade responded.

I threw my hands up in the air. "Whatever. I'm not going back and forth with you and Calvin on this. I'm tired. Tired of the drama from both of you."

Sade responded, "Mama, it hurts me to see you allow Calvin to get away with what he's done to you."

"I'm going to be okay. Couples go through some things. Calvin realizes he can't hit me every time I say or do something he doesn't like."

"When I turn sixteen, I'm going to sign up for some government programs and try to find housing for me and my baby. I refuse to bring my baby up in this environment."

"Sade, you will do no such things. Nobody is going to rent to a sixteen year old."

"I've been looking into it and when I turn sixteen, as long as I get some assistance, there are a few apartments that will rent to me."

I felt like I was having a panic attack. My chest tightened. I couldn't lose Sade. Besides Calvin, Sade was my life. I felt in my spirit if Sade left my house, Sade would never return. "What can I do to convince you to stay?" I asked.

"Mama, you already know the answer to that."

I had to do something between now and next month. My baby would be turning sixteen in the middle of next month and I couldn't bare not having Sade here with me. I needed to figure out a way for Sade and Calvin to get along. Talking the other day didn't work, so I needed to come up with another plan. If I couldn't get them to get along, I was going to lose my baby and that's something I couldn't let happen.

~32~

SADE

How's my favorite new friend?" Brandon asked, as he walked up to me a few days later.

Never thought it would be possible, but I actually blushed. "Hungry. I rushed out the house this morning before eating breakfast. I don't know if I'll be able to make it to lunch."

Brandon pulled out a bag of chips from his backpack. "You can have this if you want it."

I didn't hesitate to take it. My baby was begging for some food. It wasn't a full meal, but it was something. I opened the bag and devoured the chips as if it was my last meal.

"Dang girl, slow down," Brandon teased as we walked down the hallway.

In between bites, I said, "I told you I was hungry."

Brandon laughed. We continued to walk. Brandon stopped where the hallway split. "I got to get to the gym, but saw you and had to come speak. Sorry, I didn't get a chance to call yet, but I will tonight. You can count on it." Brandon winked his eye.

I stood and watched him walk away.

"He's mine," a familiar high-pitched voice said from behind me.

My smile turned upside down as I slowly turned around to face the sound of the voice. I came face to face with Chardonnay Hicks. Chardonnay and I was about the same height. She had naturally long black hair that hung to her shoulders. Her almond colored skin was flawless with slanted eyes; the boys loved her exotic look. There was no love lost between the both of us. We never liked each other. We've known each other since we were five years old. She used to tease me about not having a father. She acted like her having a father in the house was so much better. I couldn't see it because at the end of the day, we both stayed in the same shabby apartment complex. If my dad were alive, he would have moved my mom and me to a house a long time ago, so Chardonnay having a father didn't make her so special after all.

Although we're both teenagers now, I never forgot the teasing so I chose to keep her at arm's length. She was a frenemy.

With a sly grin on my face, I responded, "Apparently, he doesn't know it."

Chardonnay stepped closer and into my personal space. She had the nerve to look me up and down. "If you weren't in your condition, I would lay you out right here for disrespecting me."

Oh no this bitch didn't. She wanted to throw down. I got many frustrated feelings bottled up in me so we can do this. I dropped my backpack down next to her. "Bitch, don't let that stop you."

By now, a few students who were passing by stopped to view the action.

We stood eye to eye. I didn't blink and with the look in my eyes, dared Chardonnay to throw the first punch.

Chardonnay backed up. "You not even worth my time. I'm out. Remember what I said. He's mine."

I watched as Chardonnay walked away and stood near a group of other girls. They turned away their backs from me and followed behind Chardonnay. Chardonnay may be Ms. Popular here at Fair Park, but she should remember how I throw down. We've gotten into enough fights around the apartment complex growing up. I whooped her ass every single time, so pregnant or not, I was prepared to whoop her ass again as a reminder.

"I'm glad somebody stood up to Chardonnay," a soft voice said nearby.

I looked up into the face of another girl from the neighborhood, Kelly Jefferson. Kelly was petite, a little nerdy, but cool.

"She doesn't scare me," I responded.

"So how you like Fair Park?" Kelly asked.

"It's no Booker T," I responded. I had been here for over two months, but still didn't like it better than my old school.

"I hear you. I wanted to come up to you and say something before now, but you seemed to be in your own little world," Kelly confessed.

"I've had a lot on my mind," I responded. Kelly was cool and I never had beef with her, but right now, I wasn't in a sociable mood.

"I bet." Kelly looked down at my stomach. "Does your baby daddy go to Booker T?"

I brushed past the subject. I didn't have time for her twenty questions. Besides, since I don't know Kelly well, she could be asking questions so she could go blab to anyone who would listen. "Kelly, I'm late for class. I'll see you around."

"Sure, okay," Kelly responded.

I didn't lie to her. I only had a few minutes to get to my next class or I would be considered tardy. Lunchtime couldn't come quick enough for me. My stomach growled so loud during class that I'm sure others heard it. The potato chips I'd eaten earlier disappeared out of my system an hour after eating them.

The lunch bell rang and I headed straight to the cafeteria. After grabbing my lunch tray, I found an empty seat in a corner of the cafeteria. A smile swept across my face when I noticed Brandon approaching the table. He placed his tray down and sat across from me.

"I heard about what happened this morning," he blurted out as soon as he sat down.

"So, you and Chardonnay got something going on?" I asked, right before taking a bite out of my ham and cheese sandwich.

"Negative. Chardonnay is too trashy for me."

I was relieved to hear he didn't think too highly of her either. "According to her, you two are a couple. Why is she going around saying that?"

Brandon's eyes shifted away. "I hit it, once. Well, maybe twice. She thought because I sexed her that she was my girl."

"Did you lead her on to believe that she was your lady?"

"No. Chardonnay, knew what time it was. She let my boy hit it too. Wasn't no love there at all."

"So in other words, she's a lying hoe."

Brandon seemed to feel more at ease. "If you want to say that."

I continued to eat my food. "Brandon, you seem like a nice guy, but I don't know if I want to talk to a guy who slept with Chardonnay."

"I didn't realize y'all were friends."

"We're not. But if you got some unresolved feelings for her. I don't need that kind of drama in my life right now."

Brandon took my hand and looked me in the eyes. "I can assure you that I have no, meaning zero feelings for her. I fucked her and that was it. She never got the best part of me." He placed my hand over his heart.

I smiled. "Brandon, you're something else."

"That's what my mom tells me all of the time," Brandon grinned, showing his pearly white teeth. "So, will you give me a chance? Give me a chance to show you how much I like you."

Things were moving fast. I felt my heart beat faster. "Brandon, you don't know me." I looked down at my stomach. "And I have a package."

"As long as it's not a problem with you, it's not a problem with me," he assured me. "I want to get to know everything about you Sade."

I looked at Brandon. "Out of all of the girls at this school, why are you interested in me? I know I'm cute, but I'm pregnant so why?"

I'd never lacked confidence in my looks, but I wondered why Brandon wanted to talk to me knowing that I was pregnant and he wasn't the baby daddy.

Brandon responded, "Sade, normally, I wouldn't be trying to holla but there's something about you that I can't put my finger on. You seem different than some of the other girls here."

"Different how?" I tilted my head.

"Different in a good way. You don't have fake airs about yourself. You seem to be genuine. Although you do have a slight attitude." Brandon held his two fingers together to indicate how much. "I can tell you just do that to keep people away. I bet under all of that, there's a heart of gold." He smiled.

I melted. Being around Brandon calmed me. I was a little confused because the feelings that Brandon evoked in me were foreign to me. I had read about love at first sight in books, but never thought I would experience it. He made my heart flutter and my insides feel all gooey whenever he was near. My overly confident exterior only masked how nervous he really made me feel whenever he was around. With all I had going on, thinking about love should have been the furthest thing from my mind, but like the heroine in the books I read, I felt like with Brandon, it was love at first sight.

I decided to change the subject. "Do you play sports?" I asked.

"I do, but I'm not on the team. Not good enough. I do play a mean keyboard. I'm in the band."

"Really?" I asked.

"Yes. I love music." Brandon's eyes lit up.

"I do too. I love to sing."

We spent the rest of our lunch period discussing our love for music. For the first time since being here in

four months, I felt good about being at Fair Park High
School.

~33~

JOYCE

I tried to cover up the bruise under my eye with make-up. Some of my co-workers looked at me sideways when I walked in to work wearing my huge black shades. I kept them on all day because I would rather them look at me strange than to start asking me questions on why or how I got this black eye.

My manager pulled me to the side and asked, "Joyce, I don't like getting into folks business, but don't you think you should wait until you get off to put your shades on?"

"I got something in my eye and it's swollen," I lied.

"Oh okay. Well, if you must," she assured me before leaving me standing there by myself.

Embarrassed that people probably knew why I wore the shades, I kept to myself as much as I could. I was so glad when my shift ended. I rushed to my car and high-tailed it out of the employee parking lot and headed home.

After my twelve-hour shift of dodging folks, I couldn't wait to slide off my shoes from my aching feet. I placed them under the bed and massaged each one.

Calvin was not here and instead of calling his cell phone like I normally would, I welcomed the fact he was gone. These moments alone made me realize I didn't know Calvin as well as I thought I did. I knew he was nothing like Sade's dad, but I thought Calvin loved me. His actions lately have me questioning his love for me. If he loved me, why did he hit me?

We were all stressed. We're a house full of stressed people, but it didn't give him the right to put his hands on me. The more I thought about it, the angrier I got. I meant it, Calvin had better not ever raise his hand to hit me again. I refused to become another battered woman. What kind of example am I setting for Sade if I allowed the abuse to continue? This time, better be the last time.

Someone knocked on the front door. I wasn't expecting company. "Sade, are you in there?"

I got no response from Sade. I jiggled the door, but it was locked. Someone knocked on the front door again. I hoped whoever it was would go away but had no such luck as they beat yet another time.

I walked in the living room."Who is it?" I yelled.

"It's me, Sade, I forgot my key."

"Chile', don't be knocking on my door like a crazy person," I said as I opened the door.

Sade rushed past me. "Got to use the bathroom."

"Might as well cook some dinner," I said. I was tired, but hungry.

Instead of going back to my room, I went straight to the kitchen. The least Calvin could have done was take something out of the freezer for me to cook. I checked the refrigerator to see if something was thawed, but no such luck. I retrieved a package of frozen ground beef and turned on a burner. I placed the frozen meat in a skillet over the open fire.

"Where's Calvin?" Sade asked from across the kitchen.

"Not here."

"Good."

Joyce stopped preparing dinner. "Sade, watch your attitude now."

"It's just good to have my mom to myself sometimes."

Sade walked up to me and I hugged her. I pulled back and looked at Sade's protruding stomach. "Looks like you've gotten bigger in just these past few days." I rubbed her belly.

"I have. Hardly any of my clothes are fitting anymore." Sade picked up a slice of tomato.

"Young lady, wait for dinner," I said, playfully hitting her hand.

"But mama, this little one wants something now."

"It'll be done soon. I'll make you a salad while you wait on me to finish cooking. We're eating Hamburger Helper."

Sade took a seat at the table while I fixed her a plate of salad. "Mama, how's your face doing?" Sade asked after taking a few bites.

"I'm fine."

Sade didn't respond. Sade ate and I continued to cook. We were both in our own little world. The tranquil silence was broken at the sound of Calvin's voice. "Where's my favorite lady at?" he yelled.

"Right here," I responded.

Sade pushed away from the table. "Let me know when the rest of the food is ready."

"Sade, you don't have to leave." She and I had a peace between us until Calvin came and ruined it. I wished Calvin had stayed gone longer.

"I'm out of here." Sade brushed past Calvin when he entered the kitchen.

Calvin walked up to me, bent down, and kissed me on the lips. "Hi, baby," he said, afterwards.

The frown on my face remained. "Where have you been, Calvin?"

"Out looking for a job. Didn't you tell me I needed a REAL job?" Calvin emphasized the words real and job.

"Any luck?" I asked, as I stirred in the noodles and other ingredients.

"Baby, it's hard out there. Don't expect me to get something quick, but at least I'm trying."

My back was to Calvin so he couldn't see me roll my eyes as I listened to him go on and on about his day of looking for a job.

Doing my best to sound supportive, I said, "You put in a lot of applications, so hopefully, someone will call."

"That's what I love about you, Joyce. You have confidence in your man." Calvin placed his arm around my waist. "I love you, baby."

"Love you too," I mumbled. It was hard staying mad at Calvin; especially when he was in close proximity.

Calvin turned me around and kissed me passionately. When I opened my eyes, the little joy I felt disappeared. Staring at me from the doorway was Sade with a disappointing look on her face.

~34~
SADE

Just when I thought my mom was going to kick Calvin to the curb, he would say something smooth or clever and work his way back into her good graces. I originally came to the kitchen to get me something to drink, but after seeing them two kiss, I changed my mind. I broke eye contact with my mom and went back to my room.

I watched television until my mom yelled from the other side of the door that dinner was ready. I washed up and fixed my plate. I sat at the table, but remained quiet. The sound of Calvin's fork scraping his plate irritated me. His loud smacking didn't help either. It was like he was purposely trying to get on my nerves.

"How's school baby?" my mom asked.

"Fine," I responded.

"Maybe after you have the baby, you can re-apply to Booker T. It doesn't mean you have to give up on your dreams," she said.

I doubted I would be able to get back in. "Me and the girls are going into the studio next month," I said.

"Word. Well, don't forget about me and your mama," Calvin said.

"Mom, can we talk after dinner?" I looked at Calvin and then back at my mom. "Alone."

"Sure. Just let me wash these dishes afterwards and I'll come to your room."

After dinner, I went to my room and retrieved my diary from underneath the mattress. For the first time in a long time, I drew a smiley face in my diary entry. I wrote about Brandon and how sweet he was. My face frowned when I thought about the last part of my day though. The last few sentences weren't happy thoughts at all. I wrote about how everything Calvin did would irritate me.

"Knock. Knock. Can I come in?" my mom asked before opening my unlocked door.

I closed my diary and placed it under my pillow as she walked closer. I looked up at her. "Mom, I'm not trying to put any more pressure on you, but I need to say something, but I don't know how."

"Spill it. I don't have all day." She folded her arms in defense.

I'd been reading some magazines and they suggested if you had a problem with someone that you should confront the person. I loved my mom, but I also found myself getting upset with her about things. I glanced at the floor. "I feel like you haven't been there for me."

"You're fifteen years old and can take care of yourself."

I got the nerve up to now look at her in the eyes. "But you're still my mama and now I'm pregnant."

"Didn't nobody tell you to go out and get yourself pregnant." She kept her arms folded, but started tapping her foot.

"I don't know why I thought talking to you would do any good. If it's not about your precious Calvin, you don't care."

She unfolded her arms, walked, and sat down on the edge of my bed. "Baby, that's really not true. I do care about you."

"I don't feel like you do." I had promised myself I wouldn't cry, but felt myself getting teary-eyed.

"When you become an adult, you'll understand. Calvin's my husband and you're my daughter. I'm trying to do the best I can."

"I need you, Mom. Do you know how hard that is for me to admit that to you after you continue to take up for that man?"

"That man is your stepfather and you need to show him respect." She reached out to me.

I pushed her hand away. "Apparently Calvin didn't knock any sense into you."

My mom raised her hand to slap me, but stopped inches away from my face. I stared at her with disbelief. It never failed. My mom broke my heart again. I pulled my legs up as close as I could to my protruding belly.

I guess she felt remorseful because she said, "I'm sorry. I didn't mean to."

"I hate you!" I yelled. "I hate you!"

"I'm sorry, Sade. Please forgive me."

"You're not my mama. You can't be."

She ran out of the room crying. I wanted her to feel the pain I felt. My body shivered from anger. I held on to the anger to mask the pain I felt.

My cell phone rang. I picked it up without looking at the caller ID. "What?" I snapped.

"Who pissed you off?" Brandon asked from the other end of the phone.

My voice softened. "I've had a bad night."

"What can I do to make it better?" Brandon sounded sincere.

"I wish there was something you could do, but its family problems."

"I can relate to that." Brandon went on to tell me about some of his issues. He was the youngest of three boys. His other two brothers were both locked up in the state penitentiary. He was dealing with his mother and her drug abuse problem. "Everyone's expecting me to screw up and end up like my brothers. I refuse to prove them right."

I admired Brandon's drive. I confessed, "Well, I'm the only child. My mom married my worst nightmare and there's nothing I can do about it."

"Can you go live with your dad?" Brandon asked.

"I wish. My dad died when I was a baby."

"Sorry to hear that Sade. If you want to talk about it, I'm a good listener."

I decided to change the subject. "How long have you been playing the keyboards?"

We went back and forth about some of our favorite things with music being one of many things we both had in common. Two hours later we got off the phone. I smiled and Brandon was the last thing on my mind as I drifted off to sleep.

"No, no," I screamed. Calvin was touching me all over my body and I was trying to stop him. I woke up realizing it was only a dream. I closed my eyes and attempted to go back to sleep, but failed. No matter how hard I tried to escape, Calvin seemed to be right there in my mind to remind me there was no escaping him.

~35~

JOYCE

Sade and I were at the doctor's office. I watched the doctor place the probe on Sade's stomach. Sade's accusation the week before hit a nerve. As much as I wanted to deny Sade's comments, I had to face the fact that there was truth in Sade's words. I was guilty of not spending much time with her lately. My baby girl was pregnant and if I were to face the truth head on, no, I hadn't been there for her in a way a mother should.

After arguing with Calvin over the weekend, I vowed to change things. I needed to work on repairing my relationship with Sade. Sade didn't know it, but I planned to throw her a surprise sweet sixteen party.

The doctor said cheerfully, "Sade, looks like you're having a girl."

Tears flowed down Sade's face. I did what any other mother would do. I got tissue out the nearby box and wiped her tears. "It's okay, baby. We're going to take real good care of her."

The doctor said, "Sade's coming along great. Being eight months pregnant, everything looks fine so far. See."

We both looked at the monitor and saw the baby move in her stomach. The doctor printed out a photo of the sonogram and handed it to Sade. After Sade dressed, I signed some papers at the front desk and we left out of the clinic.

"Mama, I don't know if I'm ready for this," Sade confessed on the ride back home.

"We're going to get through this together. You, me and Calvin," I responded.

"That's just it, mama. After I have the baby, I'm not coming back unless Calvin is gone. I mean that."

While watching the traffic, I partially watched Sade from the corner of my eye. "Dear, you don't know anything about raising a child. I'll be there to help you and I can't do that if you're living somewhere else."

"Mom, I'm trying not to disrespect you, but that's final. Either he goes or my daughter and I go."

Sade was adamant about leaving and I was adamant about trying to keep my family together. We were at a standstill so we rode the rest of the way lost in our own thoughts. When we got to the apartment, Sade headed straight to her room. I went to my room and as usual, Calvin wasn't anywhere around. Frustrated, I decided to go wash up and cook dinner.

SPARKLE

I turned the knob on the bathroom sink. Nothing came out. "What in the world?" I said. I went to the kitchen sink and turned the knob. Nothing. Not a drop of water came out.

I immediately called the water company only to learn that the water was cut off because the bill hadn't been paid in two months. I'd given Calvin the money to pay the bill so after arguing with the customer service representative for a few minutes; I realized she was telling me the truth. I hung up with her and then called the toll free number to my bank. After calculating to make sure there would be enough funds to cover the water bill, I called the water company back and paid the bill over the phone.

The customer service representative said, "We'll send someone out to turn it back on before the end of the day. You have a nice day."

Disgusted that I had just spent the money on an unexpected expense, I dialed Calvin's number. As usual, he didn't answer. I didn't bother to leave a message. Cooking dinner was out. I grabbed my keys and left the apartment. I used my last ten dollars I had in my pocket to buy Sade and me a meal from a nearby hamburger joint.

When I got back to the apartment, I went to Sade's room and handed her the meal and I went back to the living room to eat mine. Calvin hadn't returned my

call nor was he back at home. After eating, I tried to concentrate on the show on television, but failed.

Several hours later, Calvin waltzed in as if he didn't have a care in the world. He was humming, smiling, and tried to kiss me. I blocked his kiss with my arm.

"What in the hell did you do with my money?" I yelled.

"Baby, calm down. I don't know what you're talking about."

I threw the water bill I had found still in the drawer at him. "Do you remember not paying the water bill? I came home this evening and went to wash my hands and guess what--no water."

Calvin yelled, "Hold up. I know I paid that bill." He left the living room and headed to the kitchen. He returned to the living room. "The water's on, so what the hell you talking about Joyce?"

"Of course it's on. I paid it via the phone today so it's supposed to be on. Fortunately, the rep didn't charge me a reconnect fee."

Calvin couldn't even look me in the eyes. "What had happened was, I stopped by Marcus house, and a crap game was going on. I thought I could double our money, you know so you wouldn't have to worry about next month's bill."

I threw my hand up in the air. "Save it. Two months, Calvin. The bill hadn't been paid in two months. That's why they cut it off when they did."

"I lost okay. I tried to recoup it again this month."

I shook my head from side to side. "I make the money and all you have to do is go pay the bill, but no you can't even do that."

"Joyce, I understand you're upset, but you better watch how you talk to me."

"Or what? You're going to hit me again. I don't think so. Because I told you Calvin if you ever…and I do mean ever raise your hand to hit me again, it would be the last time."

Calvin leaned his head back and laughed. "You have lost your mind. I'm the only one wearing the pants in this house and you're going to obey me."

Calvin raised his hand up to hit me. I jumped up off the couch, but wasn't fast enough. Within seconds, Calvin had pounced on me, using his fists to attack my body. I used my arms to shield my face. I felt that if I could protect my face, I would be all right. With each punch to my body, I felt weaker and weaker I couldn't believe the man that I loved would do me like this. Tears flowed down my face as I faded to black.

~36~
SADE

I heard the commotion between Calvin and my mom from my room. I stayed in my room with the door closed until I heard the front door slam. Soon as I heard Calvin leave, I rushed out and saw my mom passed out on the couch.

"Mama, mama," I said as I shook her. A bruised up Joyce laid out on the couch.

She wouldn't wake up. I tried not to panic. I got up and dialed nine-one-one. I confirmed the address with the operator. I cradled my mom in my arms until I heard a knock on the door. It had taken them long enough. It had been fifteen minutes since I placed the call. I tried not to think about that as I opened the door for the paramedics.

I grabbed my mom's purse and followed behind the paramedics. The paramedic tried to assure me that she would be okay on our way to the hospital. "We think she suffered a concussion. Do you know who did this?" the man asked.

"Calvin Thomas."

"We'll need all of his information so we can tell the police."

"The police?" I asked. I didn't know if I should get the police involved. I didn't want Calvin to take out his anger on my mom again.

"Yes. We had to report this. They will be waiting at the hospital. Soon as we get your mom admitted, they will probably want to ask you a few questions."

I said a silent prayer for my mom's recovery as we rode quickly down the freeway to the hospital. Just as the paramedics had said, there was a police officer there waiting to ask questions about the incident.

Since my mom came in by ambulance, we didn't have to wait in the waiting room like others; they immediately took her to one of the emergency patient rooms. The police cornered me and asked me question after question. I tried to dodge the questions until I knew how my mom was first.

"How is Calvin Thomas related to you?" one of the officers asked.

"He's not. He's my mom's husband," I responded.

I heard my mom yelling out and left the officers still trying to figure out what happened.

"What's going on?" my mom said in a groggy voice, as soon as she saw me walk through the door. .

"Mama, I'm just glad you're awake," I responded.

She attempted to sit up, but fell back down on the hospital bed. "Yes, but where am I? Oooh, my chest is killing me."

"We're at the hospital."

"Is Calvin talking to the doctor?"

"Are you serious?" I asked in shock." Calvin's the reason why you're here. I called nine-one-one. Calvin's ghost."

"All I remember is..." she cried out in pain. "Oh my God. I can't believe I passed out."

"He tried to beat you to death and the police are outside waiting to find out what happened. Mama, we can finally get rid of him. I'll tell them everything; you don't even have to talk."

I stood up to go back outside. She grabbed my wrist. "Don't. Let me talk to them."

"Mama, you can barely talk. I'll handle this."

"No, I said. You stay out of this."

"Fine," I agreed. "I'll be right back. I'll let them know you're awake."

I stood in the background as the doctor and female police officer entered the hospital room. The doctor said, "Ms. Washington, you tried to give us a scare."

My mom's attempt at smiling turned to a look of pain as she shifted in the bed. "What's my prognosis?"

"You're lucky nothing was broken. You have a bruised rib and kidney, but we're still testing to make sure there's no internal bleeding."

"I feel like an eighteen wheeler ran over me."

"I'll have the nurse administer some pain medicine, but you're going to feel a little uncomfortable these next few days."

After the conversation with the doctor, the officer who had been quiet the entire time made herself known. "Ms. Washington, I'm Officer Parish. I need to ask you a few questions. Your daughter told the paramedics that a Calvin Thomas did this to you. Is that true?"

My mom looked at me and then back at the officer. "My daughter wasn't there when it happened."

"Okay, but that's not what I asked you Ms. Washington. Is it true that your husband did this to you? If so, we can charge him with assault. I just need you to confirm and I'll file a report."

My mom looked away. "I can't."

"You can't what, Ms. Washington?"

"I don't remember, okay. I don't remember who did this?"

"Mama, you know Calvin did this. Why don't you tell her so she can arrest him and get him out of our house now," I pled.

"Ma'am, I'm here to help you. When they realized this might be a case of domestic violence, I was called out. I've been where you are."

My mom and I both looked at the officer.

Officer Parish continued, "Yes, I know. Hard to believe, isn't it? Well, if I can get out of a two year abusive relationship, then ma'am, so can you." The officer looked in my direction." If you don't do it for yourself, do it for your daughter. From the looks of things, she's going to need her mom around to help her. Don't you want to see your grandchild?"

My mom wouldn't look the officer in the face. "I have nothing more to say."

The officer pulled out pamphlets on domestic violence. She tried to hand them to my mom, but my mom wouldn't take them. Instead, she turned her head away. The officer laid them on the bed. "I'm going to leave these here." She walked up to me. "Here's my card."

I took the card and put it in my pocket.

The officer said, "If either one of you need me for anything, don't hesitate to call me. The station's number is there and my cell phone."

"Thanks," I said.

The officer walked towards the door. She stopped and turned around. "Ms. Washington, he's never going to stop. The next time, you might not be so lucky. The next time, we are called out, it might be too late. Just something to think about. You ladies try to enjoy the rest of your day." She looked at me again. "Take care of your mom and that baby you're carrying."

As soon as the officer was out of the door, my mom used her hand and knocked the pamphlets to the floor. "Who does she think she is? She doesn't know my situation. I don't remember Calvin hitting me so why would I turn him in for assault."

I looked at my mama and then at the papers on the floor. I walked over and bent down as best as I could and picked them up. I held them in my hand.

My mom said, "I don't want them. Throw them away if you want."

I threw the pamphlets in the trash and exited the hospital room. I left to see if I could catch the officer. "Officer Parish," I yelled out.

The elevator door opened and the officer turned around and saw me. She let the elevator door close. "Young lady, is your mom ready to talk?" Officer Parish asked.

"No, ma'am. She won't talk, but Calvin, her husband, did beat her. This isn't the first time either. She does know he did it, she's just telling you she can't remember."

Officer Parish frowned. "Without her being willing to confirm it, I'm sorry there's nothing we can do."

I knew that would never happen. Without further discussion, I watched the officer get on the next elevator. Once again, I felt like I was in a hopeless situation.

~37~

JOYCE

I remained in the hospital for two days and not once did Calvin come visit me. He called the hospital room to check on me, but if Sade answered the phone, she wouldn't put the call through.

The only reason why I was on the phone with him now was that Sade had stepped out of the room to go get her something to eat in the cafeteria. Sade walked in the room while I was ending the call with Calvin. Once I had hung up, I said, "I told you need to stay out of grown folks business. This thing between Calvin and me is just that--between us. It has nothing to do with you."

"Mama, you heard the officer. He's not going to stop. It's only going to get worse. I don't want to lose you."

"Baby, you're not going to lose me. This is just something that he and I are going through. We're

going to work this out and things will get back to how they used to be."

"I'm so sick and tired of you making excuses for him. He's a molester and an abuser and you keep making it seem like he's just having a bad day."

"Sade, hold your voice down. I don't want everybody all up in my business."

"Too late. Everybody knows that Calvin is whooping that behind and you won't do a thing about it."

"Sade, you better be glad I'm in a hospital room and you're pregnant or I would beat your behind for you talking to me like this."

"I wish you would take that attitude with Calvin and just maybe you wouldn't be in this condition," Sade said, before storming out of the room.

I'm at my wits end. I didn't know what to do with Sade. Sade was getting sassier and sassier the further along in her pregnancy she got. I've tried to be understanding because with her being pregnant, her hormones were probably all over the place, but as soon as she had that baby, I would not be tolerating disrespect.

I eased myself into my clothes. I called Calvin back so he could pick me up, but he hadn't returned my call. It took all of my strength to bend down and put on my shoes. My ribs hurt. I moaned in pain.

"Hey, mama, look whose here," Sade said as she burst in the room with Maddie, Crystal's mom right behind her.

"Hi, Maddie," I said.

Sade rushed over and helped me with my shoes.

"Joyce, Sade told me what happened. I know the last time we talked we were both a little heated. I'm not going to let you go through this alone. I'm here to take you wherever you want."

"I want to go home," I said.

"Are you sure?"

"Yes." I turned to Sade. "Thank you, baby. Now can you go out and tell the nurse my ride's here so I can get out of here? I hate hospitals."

"Mama, you work at a hospital," Sade said.

"I know. That's why I hate them."

We all laughed. I stopped laughing because it hurt my chest to laugh. Sade left out to get the nurse.

"Good to see you still got your sense of humor," Maddie commented.

I pushed my pride to the side and said, "Thanks for coming."

"Let's forget that it ever happened." Maddie assisted me and helped me sit further up in the bed.

With the events of the last few days, the tension between Sade and me and the pain I was in, I couldn't hold it together any longer. I broke down crying. "Maddie, I don't know what to do. I never thought it

215

would get to this. I don't know what to do. On one hand I love him, but this." Joyce looked down at her bruised body. "This here isn't love."

Maddie rushed to my side and placed a gentle hand on my back to comfort me. "I can have Frank meet us at your place and you can tell Calvin to get his stuff and leave."

"That's just it, Maddie. I don't want Calvin to go. What's wrong with me? Why can't I let him go?" More tears flowed down my face. Something had to be wrong for me to let this man do this to me. He was causing me pain and the fact that I loved him was causing a divide between my daughter and me.

"You have to or it could be deadly."

"Don't say that."

Maddie looked down at me. I could see the disappointed look on her face, but I could also see the concern. "What more has to happen? He's beating you. He's molesting your daughter. What else does he have to do before you get that man out of your life?" Maddie asked.

Before I could respond, Sade and a nurse walked in the room. The nurse said, "Ms. Washington, someone told me you were ready to go."

Maddie handed me a tissue. I wiped my face. "Yes, ma'am. I'm ready."

"Well, I'm here to take you to your waiting chariot," the friendly nurse said.

SPARKLE

During the ride home, Maddie reminded me of why we were friends. She always had a way of making you forget your problems. She got me caught up on the neighborhood gossip. I'm sure I was part of the gossip too, but Maddie kept that tidbit to herself.

Maddie helped Sade get me to the apartment. "If you need me for anything, call me. I mean it."

"Hey, Maddie. Long time no see," Calvin said as if everything was cool.

Maddie was startled and so was Joyce when they heard Calvin's voice come up behind Maddie.

"Hey, Calvin. I was just going. Take care of your wife. She needs plenty of tender, loving care."

"Oh, I'm going to handle mine. Believe that," Calvin said, with a smug look on his face.

"Joyce, I got to go. Call me if you need anything." Maddie turned and left.

I wanted to scream out to Maddie not to leave, but knew that I couldn't. Seeing Calvin brought up the memory of him beating me. When I looked into his face, I no longer saw the man I loved and adored, he looked like an animal, a beast. The smile that was once sexy to me, seemed like it was mocking me, as he walked to the bed and bent down to kiss me.

I turned my head and Calvin's lips landed on my cheek. "Glad you're home. I've missed you," he said.

"I couldn't tell."

"You know how I feel about hospitals," he responded.

I opened my mouth to respond, but knew it was useless to say anything to Calvin. Calvin was all about self. Too bad it took me marrying him to figure that out. Instead, I leaned back on the pillow and drifted off to sleep.

~38~

SADE

At eight months pregnant, boys should have been the last thing on my mind, but I couldn't stop thinking about Brandon. He had become a very important part of my life these last few months. Because of issues that had nothing to do with him, I couldn't trust my feelings, but I simply adored him. We talked on the phone every day and met before school, during lunch, and after school before my bus left every day.

Brandon caught me off guard one night over the phone. "Sade, I know there are probably a lot of guys still trying to hit on you."

"That would be a negative," I responded.

"I'm surprised. You're one of the most beautiful girls in the school."

"Uh oh. What do you want Brandon?" I asked as I polished my fingernails.

"I want you to be my girl," he responded.

I messed up my nails. This was the last thing I expected him to say. Was I dreaming? "Brandon, I'm

pregnant. What would it look like you with a pregnant girlfriend?"

"I don't care what other people think. They can't tell me how I feel or how to live my life. Sade, I really like you and I want you to be my girl."

"I'm going to be honest with you, Brandon. I've never really had a boyfriend before."

"How could that be? You're pretty. You're smart. I don't believe you."

I responded, "I've never had a real boyfriend. Sure, guys have tried to push up on me, but none have ever asked me to be his girlfriend."

I couldn't bring myself to tell Brandon the real reason why I had never had a boyfriend. Because of the things Calvin did to me, until recently, I never had a desire to be tied down to one boy. Plenty of boys tried to get with me, but I made it a point to keep them at a distance. Something about Brandon wouldn't allow me to treat him like the others. I wanted Brandon close. I couldn't believe I was about to do this, but before I could lose my nerves, I said, "Brandon, I'll be happy to be your girl."

"Yesss!" Brandon yelled from the other end of the phone. "I promise to make you happy."

"You already have." If Brandon only knew how happy he made me. I smiled.

"My dad's letting me use his car this weekend, so Friday after school, let me take you home...well out for a burger or something and then home."

"It's a date," I responded.

My mom walked in the room. I don't know how long she had been listening to my conversation. She said, "Young lady, you're too young to be dating."

"Brandon, let me call you back." Without waiting for him to respond, I hung up the phone.

"Mom, I'll be sixteen in two weeks. Besides Brandon is just not any ol' body. He's my boyfriend."

She exhaled. "It's about time you told me who your baby's daddy is."

"No, mom. You got it twisted. Brandon is just my boyfriend. And for the record he and I have never had sex."

She said, "I don't know if this is a conversation I want to have."

"Well, you assumed he was the daddy, so I'm just making it clear"

"I need you to meet Maddie downstairs and pick up the prescription she got for me."

"Is she out there now?" I asked.

"She'll be here in about ten minutes."

"Why can't Calvin do it?"

"Young lady, either you're going to do it or not."

"Mom, I'm going to do it. I'm just saying. You all up in my kool-aid about Brandon so I'm trying to

figure out why Calvin can't go pick it up from Ms. Maddie or why Ms. Maddie even had to go get your medicine in the first place."

"Sade, just go get my medicine from Maddie, please."

I didn't speak back this time. I did as I was told. I thought about Brandon. He seemed to be totally opposite of Calvin. Brandon's gentleness in his speech and dealings with me always made me feel at ease.

Maddie blew the horn when she pulled up in front of the apartment complex. I got up from the stoop and walked over to the car. "Hi Ms. Maddie."

"Hi Sade. Tell your mom to call me."

"Okay," I responded as I took the white prescription bag.

"How's she really doing?" Maddie asked.

"She's alright. Just in pain every now and then," I responded.

"He hasn't touched..."

Before she could finish, I cut her off. "No."

I hadn't lied to Maddie. Not since the day in the kitchen had Calvin touched me, but I didn't feel like going into that incident with her. I waved at her and then turned and walked back up the walkway. I moved slowly up the stairs for two reasons. The baby was kicking and caused me a little discomfort and because I dreaded going back into the lion's den.

~39~

JOYCE

I stood in the hallway right outside the living room and watched Sade and Brandon interacting with one another. This was the first boy Sade had openly showed interest in so I was curious to see what type of boy would date a girl that was clearly pregnant with another boy's child.

I decided to make myself known so I cleared my throat and walked in the living room. Sade and Brandon both looked in my direction.

Sade said, "Brandon, this is my mom." Sade looked at me. "Mom, this is Brandon."

Brandon stood up and extended his hand. I shook it. "Nice to meet you."

He has manners, I thought. I responded, "Nice to meet you too, Brandon. Have y'all eaten anything?"

"Yes, we stopped at Mickey D's," Sade responded.

That's when I noticed the empty wrappers that had once contained food. "Brandon, tell me about you."

I took the liberty of taking a seat in the chair as I waited for him to respond.

Brandon looked directly at me. "Not much to tell. My parents are divorced. I have two brothers. I'm the baby of the family and I live with my mother not too far from here."

"What's your mom's name? I might know her," I said.

"Katherine Moss," Brandon responded.

"Katherine Moss," Joyce repeated. "I don't know her, but maybe we'll get to know each other now that you and my daughter are dating."

"Mom!" Sade said.

"I'm just saying. Anyway, Brandon, it's nice to meet you. As long as you keep Sade happy, I'm happy. Understood."

"Yes ma'am. You don't have to worry about a thing. I'm crazy about your daughter."

I noticed the gleam in Brandon's eyes when he looked at Sade. "Y'all go ahead and do what y'all were doing. I'm going to go back to my room and relax a little."

Once I was snuggled under my covers, it didn't take long for me to doze off to sleep. I felt the bed shaking. I woke up. "Calvin?" I asked as I opened my eyes.

"Did you know that Sade had a man in the house?"

"He's seventeen years old. He's still a kid and yes, I knew."

"She's too young to be dating," Calvin snapped.

"She's about to be sixteen and she's about to be a mama so I think we're a little too late to worry about boys." I stretched and then sat up in the bed.

"That boy is not welcomed here."

"Brandon seems to be a nice young man and I don't want my daughter sneaking off to meet him, so Calvin, he can come over here anytime he wants. As long as it's during decent hours."

"Not if I have anything to do about it."

Calvin marched towards the door. I got up and raced behind him. "Calvin, what are you doing?"

"I'm going to tell him to leave my house."

"The last time I checked, this was 'our' home so I say he stays. If you go out there and embarrass Sade, I promise you I will not forgive you."

Calvin stopped and hesitated. "Fine. When she ends up getting hurt, I don't want to hear you moaning about it." Calvin turned back around and walked to his side of the bed.

Sade seemed to have some form of happiness with Brandon. I hadn't been too good at making her happy lately so I refused to let Calvin take that away from Sade. Until I could figure out how to get them to squash the beef between them, I would try to keep them apart and happy separately.

***

Maddie and I sat across from each other in the living room. Maddie said, "You're looking much better."

"I feel better too. I'm glad I was able to get a few more days off. I think my body needed the rest." I poured us both a drink.

"How's Calvin been acting?"

"Oh, he got some act right. He must realize I'm not going to take no more of his abuse." I don't think Maddie believed me, but it sounded good.

Maddie gulped down her drink and held her glass out for another refill. "Fill her up."

I did just that and an hour later, we had drank an entire bottle of rum.

"That's some good stuff there," Maddie's words slurred.

"Maddie, can I confess something to you?" I said. I stood up, but felt a little dizzy, so I plopped back down on the sofa.

"Confessions are good for the soul. Well that's what they tell me." Maddie burst out laughing.

"I think Calvin's cheating on me. He's hardly ever here. He's supposed to be paying the bills, but things have been being cut off. I think I made a huge mistake marrying him."

"Well, hallelujah. She finally woke up." Maddie threw her hands up in the air.

"Maddie, I'm serious. I'm not joking. I've made a huge mistake and its tearing me apart."

"My cousin's boyfriend sister is a lawyer. I can get her number for you so you can start the divorce proceedings."

"Hold up. Who said anything about divorce? Besides, I can't afford no attorney."

Maddie sat up. "Didn't you just say you made a mistake? I thought you wanted to correct it."

"I said I made a mistake. I didn't say I wanted to end my marriage. I take my vows seriously. It says until death do us part and that's exactly what I plan on doing."

"Until your death.'Cause if you stay with him, as sure as my name is Maddie Jackson, that man of yours is going to kill you."

Maddie's words sobered me up. "Maddie, are you okay to drive home? It's getting late. Calvin will probably be here any minute and since you two don't seem to like each other, it's probably best you get going."

"Are you kicking me out?" Maddie gathered her purse and keys.

I lied. I really wanted her to go. "Of course not."

I had gotten rid of Maddie just in the nick of time. Fifteen minutes after Maddie left, Calvin walked in

the apartment. I could smell the liquor on Calvin's breath as he approached my side of the bed.

"Brush your teeth first." I eased my head back.

"You know you want this." Calvin pulled me towards him and kissed me anyway. "Looks like I'm not the only one whose been drinking."

I wiped my mouth. "But, my breath doesn't stink. Please, go brush your teeth or at least gargle with some mouthwash."

"Fine. Anything to please you, baby."

"Yeah, right," I said under my breath as he walked out of the living room towards the bathroom. I wanted him to brush his teeth because I had no idea who he was with or what he was doing, but one thing was for sure, tonight he wouldn't be doing me because as soon as I laid my head on the pillow, I was out cold.

~40~
SADE

From the outside of the building, it looked like a regular office building. No one would have suspected that inside was a state of the art studio manned by one of Dallas's hottest music producers, Manchu. He sat behind the console while Crystal, Dena, and I went into the sound booth.

I stood behind the microphone and sang, "Ooh boy, I love you so. Making me want to never let you go."

Crystal repeated the note by singing, "Let you go."

Manchu turned on the intercom. "Sade, I need for you to hold the word go and then Crystal you come in with 'let you go.' Let's try it again."

We did as we were told. At the end of recording those stanzas, Dena spit out her verse of rhymes.

Manchu said, "Give me about fifteen minutes, and I'll let y'all hear something. Food and drinks in the back."

Jada said, "Ya'll that song is on fire. Sade, you got some chops girl."

I beamed with pride. I was thinking of Brandon when I wrote those lyrics. Manchu read the lyrics and came up with the perfect beat. Fifteen minutes later, Manchu played the song over. "That's it," Dena yelled.

Manchu agreed. "Ladies, let me work on this a little and we got something to take to the record company. This sounds like a hit to me."

We gave each other high-fives. Manchu said, "Watch it lil' momma, don't want to hurt your baby now."

I responded, "I still have about two more months."

"You hope. Looks like your stomach got bigger overnight," Jada said.

"I know. It feels like it too." I rubbed my stomach.

"Hey, little one. Your auntie Dena is going to spoil you." Dena rubbed my stomach.

"Can we get a copy of the song?" Jada asked.

Manchu said, "I'm really not supposed to do that, but since this is your first and I know you young ladies are excited, I will, but on one condition."

"What? We'll do anything?" Crystal answered for all of us.

"You can't make copies. We don't want to chance someone making bootleg copies and selling them on the streets. Our goal is to get Adore on the radio and people buying your music legitimately."

SPARKLE

Manchu made us all copies of the song and we couldn't wait to hear how it sounded on Jada's booming system. We rushed to the car. Jada blasted our song in the car as soon as she got behind the steering wheel. "Man, we're going to be rich," Jada said as she rocked to the song as she drove.

"It sounds just as good or if not better than the songs K104 is playing," Dena said.

I listened to them talk about our new song while Brandon and me began to text each other back and forth. Jada dropped Dena off first and then me. Brandon was waiting outside of my apartment complex when we pulled up.

"Who is that cute boy there?" Jada asked as she eased the car up behind Brandon's father car.

Brandon was leaning on the car looking like a tall, dark piece of chocolate. Chardonnay stood nearby.

"That's our girl's new boyfriend," Crystal said.

"Introductions, pleassse," Jada said.

"Stop drooling over my man," I said while taking off my seatbelt.

"He's fine. Does he have any brothers?" Jada asked.

"Yes, but they locked up." I grabbed my backpack.

"When they getting out?"

Crystal said, "Girl, forget Jada. Better get your man before that heifer there tries to steal him."

"I'm not worried about Chardonnay."

Jada said, "I wouldn't trust her."

"Don't nobody want Char. Believe me, I already peeped her game. And when it comes to Brandon, she can keep it moving."

I exited the car and walked over to Brandon. Brandon wrapped his arm around my waist as much as he could under the circumstances.

Chardonnay rolled her eyes. "Oh, I didn't know you were here to see her."

Brandon said, "I told you why I was here. Stop tripping."

"Whatever. I don't want you no way. He's all yours," Chardonnay said as she stormed up the walkway into the apartment complex.

"She's a trip."

Brandon grabbed my hand. "Forget her. Let me hear that song you were telling me about."

I removed the CD out of my backpack and handed it to him. Brandon held the passenger door open. I eased my big belly and me inside. He rushed to the driver's side and got in. "We can listen to it while I go get you something to eat."

Even if I weren't the one singing the song, I would have liked it. "You like?" I asked.

Brandon smiled. "Sade, this is good. This sounds so professional. It's good. I think others will like it too."

"Liking it is one thing, but do you think people will love it. Want to request it on the radio. Want to see a video."

"Sade, all of the above. I think your group Adore is going to blow up."

"Really? Well, we'll need a band. Somebody to do our clothes. Our makeup." I was excited and spurting out things that I had dreamed about while going to Booker T.

"I got the band. And I'm sure you'll figure out the other stuff," Brandon assured me.

"So you really think we're on to something?" I asked again.

"Sade, once he mix and master this song, you ladies better get ready. I think this is going to change your life."

I felt a kick in my stomach. It brought me back to reality. With me being pregnant, I wasn't too sure. I ran my hand over my belly. I had come so close to seeing my dreams come true. A lone tear fell down my right cheek.

~41~

JOYCE

I should have known something was up when people looked at me sideways as I walked down the hall to my manager's office. Now, here I was sitting on the opposite side of Diane Phelps desk as she pretended to be engrossed in a manila folder she was holding.

I cleared my throat. She finally looked up to acknowledge I was there. She pulled out a yellow sheet of paper from the folder. Looked at it and then up at me. "I'm not going to beat around the bush. I'm going to get straight to the point. Joyce, we're going to have to let you go."

"You're firing me?" I asked in disbelief.

"You can say that," the manager responded.

"What am I going to do? I have bills." I stared at Diane.

"Because you've been a valued employee, we are including a six month's severance package," she said to me as she handed me the yellow sheet of paper she had pulled out of the folder.

I looked at the paper and read over it. After putting in all of these years, I was being let go. "I have enough sick time," I said. "If not enough sick leave, vacation time."

Diane said, "Your work has been subpar. The report our department is required to turn in hasn't been filled out correctly for your shifts. I've been trying to be understanding, but I have to answer to my superiors. Joyce, I really hate to let you go. I really do. Maybe, once you get your personal life in order, you can reapply. If I'm here, the job is yours."

I opened my mouth to argue the fact that I thought I was doing a good job under the circumstances, but kept my comments to myself. The situation with Calvin has now affected my livelihood. I was more pissed with myself than I was at anyone else. Besides, I knew it was no sense in arguing with now my former manager. I signed the exit paper, took the check, and stuffed it in my pocket.

I walked out of the office with a bowed head. Some of my co-workers tried to stop and talk to me, but I ignored them and kept on to my locker. Only managers in my hospital unit had offices so my stuff was kept in my locker. I found an empty box and emptied out the contents of my locker into it.

The situation could have been worse. I'm grateful Diane didn't have security come escort me out like they normally would do when terminating an

employee. At least I'd been saved from that embarrassment. I looked around as I walked out one last time. I wouldn't be returning as an employee. There were other hospitals in the city, so as soon as I pulled myself together, I would apply at one of those.

Instead of going home, I drove around Dallas for what seemed like hours. Gas was high, but I didn't care. I needed to clear my head before returning home. I still had six hours left on what was supposed to be a twelve-hour shift so it wasn't like Calvin or Sade would be expecting me home any time soon.

I drove out to White Rock Lake and watched the ducks. Coming to the water always calmed me. I closed my eyes and thought about Calvin and Sade. Calvin had become more loving these last few weeks, but still my feelings for him were not as strong as they once were.

Fortunately, he hadn't tried to hit me since the last incident, but then again, I'd been careful not to say anything I thought would piss him off either. I laughed as I thought about how my life had changed. A woman should be able to disagree with her man without worrying about him hitting her.

"Pull yourself together, Joyce," I said to myself.

I looked at the small waves in the water one last time, then walked and got back in the car. I took the long way home. I started to yell out and announce myself when I entered the apartment, but wanted to surprise Calvin. Looked like I was in for a surprise. I heard Calvin's voice from the hallway as I approached the closed bedroom door. Wrong or not, I waited outside the door and eavesdropped.

"I promise to pay your phone bill. Just give me a few days. Joyce gets paid this week and I'll get it from her."

So this is what he does when I'm not here. He's talking to some skank.

"I love you too," Calvin said to the woman on the phone, right before I burst through the door.

"You bastard. Get your stuff and get out of my house. You're taking my money and giving it to your other woman. Oh hell no. Get out now."

The stress from losing my job and now walking in on him talking to another woman made me snap. I went ballistic and started throwing Calvin's stuff out of the dresser drawers. I said every curse word that came to mind. Calvin tried to calm me, but failed at first. He finally was able to wrap his arm around my body. He repeated. "Baby, it's not what you think."

"Whatever, Calvin. I'm through."

"That was my mama. If you don't believe me, call her yourself."

I didn't believe him. "Give me your phone."

"Joyce, you know I don't like you using my phone. Use your own phone."

"Calvin, give me the phone or get the hell out of my house."

"Fine. Take it. And I want an apology."

"Whatever." I snatched the phone out of Calvin's hand. I scrolled and hit the last number dialed on Calvin's phone.

I tapped my foot as I waited for someone to answer the ringing phone. "No answer. Your trick must have known it was me calling back."

Before I could hand the phone back to Calvin, his phone rang. He reached for it, but I didn't give it to him; instead I looked at the number I had just dialed and answered it. I hit the speaker button.

"Hello," I said.

"Is Calvin still around?" Calvin's mom's voice said from the other end of the phone.

Calvin tilted his head. "Told you."

"Mama Cee. I thought you were someone else."

"Put my son on please," Calvin's mom didn't even pretend to want to talk to me.

"Here. You lucked out this time." I shoved the phone at Calvin.

"I want an apology," Calvin said. "Mom, I'll be over in a minute."

He wasn't guilty this time, but I still didn't fully trust Calvin. I picked up the clothes I had thrown on the floor and placed them back in Calvin's drawers.

"It sure sounded like you were talking to some other chick."

"You're the only chick that gets this. Believe that."

"Your mom's waiting on you so you better get going."

"So no apology?" Calvin stood in front of me and asked.

I may have been wrong this time, but I still felt Calvin was up to something. "I'm sorry."

"You're going to pay for it tonight too." Calvin laughed.

I threw one of his socks at him. He caught it with his right hand. "You don't want to keep your mom waiting."

"You're right because you know she can be a real bear when she doesn't get her way."

"Like mother, like son," I said as Calvin walked out the room.

Sade came in the room and found me on the floor still picking up stuff. "He didn't hit you, did he?" Sade asked.

"No, baby. I got mad. Threw a few things. I'm just cleaning up the mess I made."

"Oh, okay. Just checking."

"It means a lot you're trying to take up for your mama, but baby girl, I got this."

Sade left me alone to finish cleaning up. I still hadn't told Calvin or Sade that I was unemployed. They would find out soon enough.

~42~
SADE

C rystal, Dena, and I, known as the group Adore, were back in the studio working on another song. I was considered the lead singer so I sang my solo part first. I stood behind the microphone and sang, "I got love and it feels so right. I got love and its taking me through the night ..."

Dena got up to the microphone and said her part. L-o-v-e let me tell you what love means to me. You and me, baby, forever. Don't ever doubt me."

We sang our parts repeatedly until Manchu felt we got it right. "Ladies, good job. We got one more song to do and that's all the studio will need."

I was glad Brandon came to the session tonight. Seeing the smile on his face motivated me as I belt out more tunes. As I sang the last song, I thought about my life and what was happening at home. I used those emotions to set the tone for the song. I sang, "It's time. Time to let it go. You hurt me once before and I can't take no more ..."

"That's a wrap," Manchu said. "I'll get with Jada and let you all know when everything is done."

"We did it," Crystal said.

We gave each other high-fives.

I told them, "Brandon's going to drop me off. I'll see y'all later."

Crystal said, "Don't forget to stop by tomorrow evening to pick up your birthday present."

"That's right, it's your birthday," Dena rapped.

"I wish I could enjoy it," I said.

Brandon said, "I'll bring her by and then I'm going to take my baby to a restaurant."

"Ooh, that's so sweet," Jada teased.

We said our goodbyes and went to our separate destinations. Brandon eased behind the wheel and drove me home. I wobbled up the walkway with Brandon on my side. He took my house keys and unlocked the door for me.

He looked down at me and said, "Sade, be ready by seven because I want to make sure we have time for dinner and a movie. I don't want your mom getting mad at me because I'm bringing you back after curfew."

I brushed his face lightly with my hand. "I'm so lucky to have you in my life. Most guys wouldn't care about a curfew."

Brandon's hand brushed my bang. "I'm not most guys."

SPARKLE

The magnetic force between us was undeniable. Brandon bent down and kissed me. I floated as we shared our first kiss. The sensation sent a jolt through my body.

Brandon must have felt it too. "I better get going," Brandon said.

"Yes. I'm a little tired."

"I'll call you later," Brandon assured me.

I smiled as I went into the apartment. Not even running into Calvin in the hallway dampened my spirits. I went to my room, closed, and locked the door.

I pulled out my diary and wrote about today. These feelings for Brandon were foreign to me. Tomorrow, I would be turning sixteen and for the first time I was falling in love. I admitted it in writing as I wrote down my feelings in my diary. I was falling in love with Brandon and it felt like Brandon was falling in love with me too. Brandon was unlike any person I had ever met. He was a boy from the hood, but he also had the good guy thing going for himself. Brandon was a well-rounded guy and he had his attention focused all on me.

I had dozed off to sleep. My phone rang, made me jump. My diary fell to the side of my bed. I reached for the phone and smiled as Brandon sang, "Happy Birthday to you" from the other end of the phone.

"Awe, thank you."

243

"I wanted to be the first one to wish you a happy birthday. I'll see you tomorrow."

I didn't realize it was after midnight until Brandon called. He was always thinking of me and doing sweet little things to put a smile on my face. If truth be told, I felt as if Brandon loved me more than my own mother and that was sad. I shook off the bout of depression that was threatening to creep in on my birthday.

I picked up my diary from off the side of the bed and wrote a quick entry. I spoke as I wrote, "Today's my sixteenth birthday. I'm happy that Brandon called. I'm happy that he cares, but it saddens me to know that nobody else seems to care about me. I'm not ready to raise a baby. I put up a good front, but I'm scared. I feel as if I have nobody to talk to about my fears. Brandon's a boy; he wouldn't understand what I'm going through.

But today's my birthday and I'm not going to get all sentimental today. It's after midnight and I'm going to end this diary entry and go to bed. When I close my eyes, I'm going to think happy thoughts. Meaning, I won't be thinking or dreaming about you know who. If I had one wish today, it would be for you know who to be erased from my life forever. That would give me my mama back and that would make me the happiest girl in Dallas."

SPARKLE

I closed my diary and placed it under my pillow. After turning off the light, I got back in bed and attempted to get comfortable. With the baby's position in my stomach, it was hard for me to get comfortable. Once I found a spot that didn't hurt much, I closed my eyes and thought of Brandon.

The sound of my doorknob turning woke me up out of my sleep. I was scared at first, but remembered I had locked it, so I was relicved. I suspected it was Calvin trying to get in because my mom would have knocked or yelled out to me by now. Calvin turned the knob several more times, but when he couldn't open the door, he went on about his business.

Sleep evaded me now. "Happy birthday to me," I said and thanked God for not allowing Calvin to be able to get in my room.

~43~

JOYCE

I still hadn't told Calvin or Sade I lost my job. I went on about life as if things were the same. I left the house during my regularly scheduled time as if I was going to work, but instead I was filling out applications at some of the other hospitals in the Dallas area. They were both so wrapped up in their own little worlds, that neither bothered to question me when I arrived home early every day.

Calvin probably didn't notice me home early because he was rarely there anyway. If he had been, he should have noticed. Woman's intuition alerted me that Calvin was probably doing things he didn't have any business doing, but I could never catch him so I had no proof. One day I would get the proof and all hell would break loose, but today was not the day.

I laid in the bed and stared up at the ceiling. Today, my baby turned sixteen years old. Thanks to Maddie, I had a location for Sade's surprise party. I probably should be saving money since I don't know how long it'll be before I find another job, but on the other hand, a daughter only turns sixteen once and as of late, it seemed as if Sade was disappointed in me as a mother. Maybe throwing her this party with all of her friends could help mend our daughter and mother relationship.

At least that's what I hoped. In the past few days, I'd done a lot of thinking and what kept coming to the forefront of my mind didn't sit right with me. The truth hurt. I had become the type of mother who put a man before her child and for that. I was ashamed of myself.

Calvin turned around in the bed and his hand automatically draped over my waist. I lifted up his arm and moved it as I eased out of the bed doing my best not to disturb Calvin as he slept.

I went to the bathroom to wash up. I checked in on Sade, but she was still sleep. I wanted to surprise her with breakfast so I cooked some of her favorite things, omelet with grits and toast and put them on a tray.

I knocked on Sade's door with one hand and waited for Sade to open it. She was rubbing her sleeping eyes. "Happy Birthday, my butterfly," I said as I entered her room with the tray of food.

"Thank you, Mom."

"I cooked some of your favorites and you get to eat it in your room since today's your day."

"Thanks," Sade responded. Sade took the tray, walked back to her bed, and sat down.

"So what do you want to do today? I was thinking about we go get our hair and nails done."

"For real?" Sade's face lit up.

"Yes. It's been awhile since we had a mother and daughter day. Why not do it today on your birthday?"

Sade attempted to hug me, but with her huge stomach and tray being in the way, she couldn't, so we just patted each other's arms. "I already took my bath so as soon as I finish eating, I'll get dressed."

"We need to be out of here by eleven so finish eating and I'll meet you in the living room once you get dressed."

I left Sade alone and went back to my room. Calvin was seated on the side of his bed whispering something into his phone. I pretended not to care as I walked right past him and into the closet to retrieve some clothes out to wear on this day.

"Oh, I don't get a good morning," Calvin said. He now stood right behind me.

"You were on the phone. I didn't want to interrupt." I shifted the clothes on the rack until I found the outfit I wanted.

I turned around holding the hanger with a blouse and jeans on them and bumped right into Calvin. "Excuse me."

"What's up with you?" Calvin asked.

"Nothing. I'm trying to get dressed so Sade and I can get out of here."

"I'm not talking about today. I'm talking about with your whole attitude. You've been having a strange attitude with me all week."

I wanted to avoid this type of conversation today. Today was about Sade and I didn't want to ruin it with a fight with Calvin. "Look, today's my baby's birthday and I really don't want to get into this with you. I've had a lot on my mind. A lot to deal with."

"I'm your husband so why haven't you talked to me about what's on your mind?"

I stopped in front of the bed. "Have you ever thought about you may be one of the things on my mind? I can't talk to you about you."

"You should. If you have a problem with me, you need to be talking to me. Aren't you the one who's always saying how important it is for couples to communicate? Well, Joyce, communicate with me. How am I supposed to fix the problem if I don't know what's on your mind?"

I turned and faced Calvin again. "I don't want to talk about it. Today's Sade's day and she's who I'm focusing on."

"Oh, you're just going to ignore your husband. I'm your husband twenty four seven, three hundred and sixty-five."

To appease Calvin and keep down the tension, I took his hand in mine. "There's nothing for you to worry about. As long as you're doing right by me. Then all is good. Now, let me finish getting dressed."

Calvin pulled me into an embrace. "I love you woman. You make me crazy sometimes, but I love you."

"Yeah, yeah." I shifted my body in his arms.

Calvin kissed me. "What all you need me to do for her party?"

I retrieved a long sheet of paper from my purse. "Make sure you get all of this and take it over to Maddie's. Please don't let Maddie do everything. Please stay and help. As soon as we get back from getting our hair and nails done, I'll be around there."

Calvin frowned. "You sure spending a lot of money for just a birthday party. What about our bills?"

"A girl only turns sweet sixteen once and my baby or should I say our baby deserves to have a party on her special day," I responded.

"I'm not saying she shouldn't have a party, but Joyce this is a lot of stuff. Where you getting all of this money to get it?" Calvin asked.

"Don't worry about it. You're not coming out of your pocket so why complain?" I folded my arms and stared at him.

"I told you I would help you pay for it."

I held out her right hand and patted it with my left hand. "Where's it at?"

"I don't have any cash on me right now," Calvin said.

My hands fell to my side. "That's exactly what I thought. Just do what I ask, okay? I got this."

I left Calvin standing right there. He watched me walk away as I left to go to the bathroom to shower. I didn't care how Calvin felt today. Today, I'm putting my little girl first and there wasn't a thing Calvin could do about it.

~44~

SADE

This had been a wonderful birthday. My mom and I were alone, meaning no Calvin. My two BFFs, Crystal and Dena had called me earlier to wish me a happy birthday. My mom and I just got our nails polished. My mom was seated with her hands under the heating fan. My nails were completely dry so I was thumbing through a magazine waiting on her. I glanced at my hands. The long acrylic nails were painted in my favorite color of pink with sprinkles of diamonds in the polish.

I put the magazine down and glanced at myself in the mirror. The quick weave I got at the beauty shop earlier had me looking and feeling like a million bucks. The baby kicking changed my train of thought. At eight months pregnant, I felt like I was going to burst any moment.

"Let's go," Joyce said, breaking me out of my thoughts.

SPARKLE

My mom was really trying to make this day special for me, so I decided to forget about our problems and enjoy the day for what it was. It had been a very long time since we'd done something with just the two of us. It felt good.

"Mama, do you mind if I go out with Brandon tonight instead of staying at home?" I asked as she drove us home.

"No, baby. In fact, I encourage you to. You're sixteen and I know I'm going to have to let my baby go." Her eyes watered.

"Mama, I'm not going anywhere. Just a date."

"Since it's your birthday, you can stay out until one. Not five minutes after one, but one, you hear me."

"Yes, ma'am." I smiled. I sent Brandon a quick text message alerting him of my new curfew time.

Two hours later, I was in my room searching through my closet for something comfortable to wear. Although my mom had bought me some new maternity clothes, nothing seemed to fit right. I wanted to look fly although pregnant. "This sucks. It's my birthday and I can't find anything decent to wear."

After trying on several outfits, I finally found an outfit that I liked. The black skirt with stretched elastic and an oversized purple satin-like blouse didn't make me look too pregnant. I dressed and then took time to put on some make-up. I put on my favorite pair of huge jingling earrings and several bangle

bracelets. I sprayed on the only perfume that didn't make me queasy. With one last look in the mirror, I jokingly said, "Brandon, eat your heart out."

My phone vibrated. It was a text from Brandon alerting me he was sitting in my living room. I opened my bedroom door just before my mom could knock. She said, "Brandon's here. Have fun. Happy Birthday again, baby girl."

We hugged. The baby kicked me. My mom moved back. "Guess she didn't like that. She already vying for my attention," my mom teased.

"It's my day so she'll have to understand," I jokingly responded.

Brandon stood up holding a bouquet of flowers when he saw me enter the living room.

"Happy Birthday, Sade." Brandon kissed me on the cheek. "These are for you." He handed me the bouquet of multi-colored flowers.

I sniffed them. "Brandon thanks. These are beautiful."

"I'll put these in some water. You two go on and I'll see y'all later." My mom took the flowers and left the living room.

A few minutes later, Brandon and I were seated in his car. While he drove, "I asked, "Did it seem like my mom was rushing us or was it just me?"

"It was just you," Brandon responded.

SPARKLE

"Hey, I need to go by Crystal's and get the present she says she has for me."

"We will, but first I need to stop and get some gas," Brandon said. Brandon pulled up to a convenience store. "I'll be right back."

While waiting on Brandon to go in the store and pump gas, I flipped from one radio station to another. I couldn't find anything on the air that I really wanted to listen to so I hit the CD button. Music from one of my favorite artists, Usher, started to play. I bopped my head.

Brandon got back in the car and handed me a brown paper bag. "What's this?" I asked.

"Open it up and see."

I opened it up and saw several bags of lemon heads. One of my favorite candies. "Awe, how sweet? I've been trying to find these and every time I go to the corner store, they are always out."

"I know. That's why I wanted to stop here because I remembered them having some."

I reached over and squeezed Brandon's hand. "You're so good to me."

"I love you, Sade. I can't help but be good to you."

I blinked my eyes. My heart fluttered. "Did you say what I think you just said?"

"What?" Brandon asked with a quizzical look on his face.

"You said, 'I love you.' Do you mean it? Do you really love me?" I asked, holding my breath as I waited on Brandon to answer.

Brandon took my hand and placed it over his heart. "I love you, Sade. My heart beats to your rhythm."

I melted right there in my seat. I couldn't help myself. Tears of joy streamed down my cheeks. "Brandon, I love you too. I've wanted to tell you that, but was unsure of how you felt about me," I confessed.

"Never doubt my feelings for you. I've never felt like this for any other girl," Brandon responded.

"Good because I never felt like this for any other guy either."

Brandon glanced at his watch. "Where does your girl live? We'll stop by there and then its dinner."

I rubbed my stomach. "The baby and I can't wait."

Less than twenty minutes later, Brandon pulled up outside of Crystal's house. "This shouldn't take long," I said.

Brandon turned off the engine and before I could get out of the car, Brandon was on the passenger side helping me exit the car.

"I'll walk up there with you."

"You don't have to," I said.

"I know, but I want to."

We walked up to Crystal's house holding hands. I rang the doorbell and it didn't take long for Crystal to come to the door. She opened the door. "Hey girl, come on in. I got your present in the living room."

We followed Crystal into the living room. Voices from everywhere yelled out, "Surprise."

Startled, I fell back on Brandon. My mom and friends threw confetti in the air and blew horns while yelling surprise and happy birthday. I looked at Brandon and playfully hit him. "I can't believe you tricked me. You knew about this, didn't you?"

My mom walked up to me and squeezed my hand. "Of course. I wouldn't have been able to do it without him. Thanks Brandon."

"Anything for Sade, Ms. Joyce," Brandon responded.

I looked in Brandon's eyes and saw the love pouring out. I looked around the room and saw the smiles on my friends' faces. No words could describe how I was feeling. I was truly happy. My happiness was threatened however when my eyes laid on Calvin standing in the corner outside of the realm of people. His eyes seemed to glow with pure evilness as his face filled with a sinister smile. He licked his lips and blew me a kiss.

I looked around to see if anyone else had noticed Calvin's action, but they must not have because they were all talking and laughing. When I looked back in the direction where Calvin had stood, he was no longer there.

"Happy Birthday, birthday girl," Calvin said from beside me.

It caught me off guard. I lost my balance. If Brandon hadn't been standing near me, I would have slipped and fell.

"Are you okay?" Brandon asked.

I looked at Calvin and then back at Brandon. "I'm fine."

I eased to the other side of Brandon away from Calvin. I would do my best to stay away from him most of the night.

~45~

JOYCE

I beamed with pride because Sade seemed to be having a good time. Calvin kept slipping out of the room talking to whoever kept calling him on his cell phone. I tried not to concentrate on Calvin, but it was hard when I felt my heart breaking. My gut feelings told me that Calvin was seeing another woman.

Maddie handed me a beer. "Glad to see things are better with you and Sade."

"A wise woman told me I needed to make things right with my daughter while I still had a chance to."

Maddie looked in the direction of where Maddic's husband and Calvin sat. "You know what else you need to do, right?"

"Let's not go there; especially not today," I said. Maddie needed to worry about her own problems and stay out of Calvin and my relationship.

"I'll drop it for now. But I believe Sade. Sade has no reason to lie about it."

Maddie left me alone with my thoughts. Sade's reason for lying is that she wanted Calvin out of the way. Sade seemed to be jealous of the time I spent with Calvin. Those were the only explanations I could give for the disdain Sade had for Calvin.

I went in Maddie's kitchen and lit the candles on the long birthday cake trimmed in pink with the words happy sweet sixteen Sade. Calvin walked in the kitchen. "Need some help?"

"Yes. Can you hold the door for me so I won't drop this?"

"I got it, baby," Calvin said.

"No. I think it's best that I carry it in."

Calvin didn't argue with me. He held the door open. Sade's friends and the adults in attendance sang happy birthday to Sade.

"Mama, thank you," Sade said as I placed the cake on the table.

Sade then hugged me. "This has been the best birthday ever."

Those words brought joy to my heart. I smiled from the inside out. "Anything for my baby," I responded. "Now make a wish."

Sade looked at Brandon and then at me. I noticed she didn't look in Calvin's direction and that was hard since he stood right next to me. Sade bent down, closed her eyes, and blew out the candles. We all clapped.

I handed Sade the knife. "It's your birthday, so you get to cut the first slice of cake."

Sade cut off a huge chunk of cake and placed it on the saucer. "This icing is good," Sade said, while licking the icing off her fork.

"You go sit down with Brandon. I'll cut the rest of the cake," I said.

Three hours later, the party was over and I was helping Maddie clean up. "Thanks again Maddie for letting me have Sade's party here."

"To see her smile the way she did tonight, I would happily do it again."

"I haven't seen her this happy in a long time." By now, I'm sweeping the floor.

"I hope she holds on to this day because I hate seeing her sad." Maddie sounded concerned about Sade.

I was glad Maddie and I mended our friendship, but there was one secret I hadn't shared with anyone. Before I lost my nerves, I blurted out, "I lost my job."

Maddie stopped wiping off the table. "So sorry to hear that. When did this happen?"

"Earlier this week. I just hadn't felt like talking about it."

"Did they say why you were let go?" Maddie asked.

"Because of excessive absences." I decided to be upfront and it felt good talking about it with someone.

"That's messed up," she said.

"Tell me about it."

"So when were you going to tell me," Calvin said from the doorway.

I almost tripped over my own feet. I was shocked to hear Calvin's voice. I stuttered, "When I got a chance to."

Maddie looked at me and then at Calvin. "Calvin, I don't want no mess here. This is a conversation you two should be having in private."

"Oh, you best believe we'll be talking about this. I came in here to get some beer and overhear you lost your job. That's messed up. I'm your husband, but here you are confiding in her."

Maddie's husband was now standing in the room. "Calvin, now man, you won't come in my house and disrespect my wife."

"Sorry, Zeke. Didn't mean no disrespect," Calvin responded.

Zeke placed his arm around Maddie's waist to show their unity. Calvin had embarrassed me. All I wanted to do was get away. I could barely look Maddie in the face. I said, "Well, Maddie thanks again. Zeke, thank you too. Calvin, come on, it's time we get going anyway."

Calvin and I walked to the car in silence. I could tell how Calvin walked that he was still upset. I was more embarrassed at Calvin's actions than mad. I got in the car. I glanced up at Maddie's house as we pulled from behind the house. I saw Maddie peeking out of her living room window.

Calvin's loud voice rang throughout the car as he pulled off. "I'm your husband and I shouldn't have to find out you were fired by walking in on a conversation."

"I was going to tell you," I responded.

"When? When the lights get turned off or as we're being kicked out of our apartment because there's no money to pay the rent?"

"It wouldn't have gone that far."

"Now I got to go hustle to make sure the bills get paid. You losing your job is making it hard on us."

The more and more Calvin talked, the higher my blood pressure got. "I got fired because of you," I blurted out.

"Oh, don't be blaming me. I don't go up on your job and do God's knows what," Calvin yelled.

"I missed too many days of work. So yes, Calvin, it was all because of you. Satisfied now."

Calvin stopped the car at the stop sign. "So how long ago did this happen Joyce and you better not lie to me either."

"Monday."

"You've been off since Monday, but yet, you've been leaving the house everyday like you've been going to work. Are you cheating on me?"

"Calvin, of course not. I should be asking you that question."

"Woman, how many times have I told you to watch your mouth?"

"You're not my daddy. I can talk to you anyway I damn well please."

"The hell you can." Calvin rose up his hand and slapped me in the face with the back of his hand.

My face stung from the assault, but I wasn't taking this fight sitting down. I started hitting Calvin back. Calvin stopped for a few seconds because he was shocked that I hit him back. He started cursing. "You've lost your mind now Joyce. Now I'm a really beat your ass."

He swung at me. Cars were honking their horns behind us, but Calvin didn't care. If anyone was looking inside of the car, all they would see were hands flying back and forth.

"I told you not to hit me again," I said as I fought back.

Calvin and I were hitting each other, getting licks in where we could. Calvin's leg must have slipped off the brakes because we slid right into the intersection and an oncoming car crashed into my side of the car. The impact caused the car to spin around. I screamed out in pain. I saw Calvin slumped over the steering wheel with blood trickling down his forehead right before I became unconscious.

~46~

SADE

When Crystal called me to let me know that my mom and Calvin had been in a serious car accident, I started freaking out. Brandon tried to calm me down, but failed. As soon as Brandon pulled the car up in front of the hospital, I hopped out and headed through the emergency room doors.

Brandon had parked and was by my side by the time I was finally able to find out where my mom was. As soon as the nurse gave me the information I needed, I rushed to the room the nurse directed me. I heard a woman scream out Calvin's name and enter a room a few doors down from where my mom was at supposedly.

"Must be one of his women," I said to myself as we continued down the hallway.

We reached the door. I was fearful of what was waiting on the other side. Brandon squeezed my hand. "I'll be right here if you need me," he assured me.

Brandon stayed outside the room as I said a quick prayer and opened the door.

I sighed with relief when I saw my mom awake with the bed in a semi-upright position.

"Mama, I got here as soon as I found out," I said, with a tear-stained face.

"I'm okay. Just got a little bruised. That's it," she tried to assure me. "Where's Calvin?"

I was disgusted. "Screw Calvin. He's the reason why you're here."

"Sade, Calvin didn't cause the accident."

"That's not what I heard. I heard y'all were fighting in the car and he pulled out in the intersection."

She didn't deny what I said. "It was an accident."

I said, "Well, I called the officer who came up here the last time you got admitted."

"You did what? Are you crazy? What if Calvin sees me talking to the police? Where is Calvin by the way?" My mom asked question after question.

"Calvin's in the room down the hall, but guess what? He had a visitor and she didn't look like no relative to me."

"Say what?"

I responded, "I saw this woman wearing some tight jeans and low cut blouse go in his room while I waited on Brandon to park and meet me up here."

"That bastard. What room is he in because I'm going to kill him," she said as she used the remote to position her bed.

"Mama, you will do no such thing. You need to relax and forget Calvin right now."

My mom ignored me. She let the rail down and placed her feet on the floor. "Where are my shoes?" she asked. "Sade, where are my shoes?"

"Here, mama." I pulled out a pair of shoes from the bag the nurse had given me.

"Pass me that shirt," she said as she pointed to the shirt she had on earlier.

I did as I was told. "Brandon's outside. He wanted to come in and check on you."

She ignored what I had to say and asked, "What room is Calvin in?"

"He's three doors down, but mama, you need to get back in the bed."

My mom stormed out the room and down the hallway. She glanced at the nameplate and burst into the room. I wobbled behind her. Brandon followed.

The mystery woman was seated in a chair next to Calvin's bed. The look on Calvin's face was priceless to me. I was glad my mom caught the woman still in Calvin's room. Now she could see Calvin for the slime he truly was.

"Who in the hell is this?" my mom asked.

"I'm Lisa and who are you?" the woman stood up. She was a few inches shorter than my mom was, even with her three-inch heels on. Her ebony straight hair accented her dark-piercing eyes and she had a butter pecan complexion. She was cute, but not prettier than my mom was.

"I'm his wife and the only one up in here asking any questions."

"Wife?" the woman blurted.

"Yes, wife."

Calvin remained quiet as he watched the women go back and forth. "Coward," I said to myself as I watched the exchange.

"You might be his wife, but I'm his woman," Lisa boldly said.

Lisa didn't seem too worried about my mom doing anything to her, so she bent down to sit back down. My mom pounded on her and they started tussling. Brandon rushed over to break the women apart. Lisa's fresh weave was now sprawled out all over her head. "Calvin, you better get your wife before I hurt her."

Calvin responded, "Lisa, I think you better go. Tell your girls I said thank you for the teddy bear."

"Yes, Lisa, I think you better," I said, with folded arms.

"Little girl, you better stay in a little girl's place."

SPARKLE

"You don't talk to my daughter like that," My mom said, sounding out of breath. She reached for Lisa but Brandon grabbed her. "Ms. Joyce, she's not worth it."

"Calvin, I'll talk to you later," Lisa said. Lisa turned and faced my mom. "I see why he doesn't want you now. You're crazy."

I grabbed the woman by her arm. "Come on. I think you've caused enough drama."

The woman snatched her hand away. I followed Lisa outside of Calvin's hospital room. My mom could be heard cursing Calvin out.

Now that Lisa and I were alone, I said, "Lisa, since you know so much about Calvin, did you know he's the father of my baby?" I rubbed my belly so it wouldn't be no mistaken that I was pregnant.

"Say what?" Lisa stopped and said.

"You heard me. Calvin and I have been sleeping with each other for six years. He's my baby's daddy. I hope you protect your girls, because Calvin loves little girls."

Mission accomplished. I noticed the ghostly expression now on Lisa's face. I turned around and headed back towards Calvin's room. Lisa rushed past me and burst through the door. "You bastard. I don't want you nowhere near me or my children. Lose my number."

My mom was now seated in a chair near the foot of the bed. I could tell she was still upset, but she looked worned out.

"Lisa, what are you talking about?" Calvin asked. He seemed more concerned about Lisa's feelings than my mom's.

"Ask her." Lisa pointed at me and stormed out of the room.

Brandon sat next to my mom and had his arm around her attempting to console her.

Calvin looked at me with venom in his eyes and asked, "What is she talking about?"

"You should be more concerned about my mama than some trick."

"Sade, watch your mouth," Calvin snapped.

"Or what Calvin? You're going to beat me like you beat my mama."

Calvin looked at my mom. "Joyce, you better control your daughter. This IV won't keep me in this bed."

"Screw you Calvin. I'm out of here." My mom said as she got up and walked away.

"Joyce, don't walk away from me when I'm talking to you."

My mom sped out of Calvin's room with Brandon and me fast on her heels.

SPARKLE

I hated to see my mom in pain, but was glad to see her walk out on Calvin. Maybe, just maybe, that meant she was walking out of Calvin's life.

"Here, I thought my birthday had been ruined, but mom walking out on Calvin is the best birthday present ever," I said.

Brandon asked, "Sade, but that's your mom. She's in pain."

I wanted to say something, but I wasn't ready to reveal everything about Calvin. Brandon would never understand. Besides, I couldn't risk sharing the information with Brandon. He accepted my pregnancy, but would he accept the fact that Calvin was my baby's daddy? It was a chance I was not willing to take.

~47~

JOYCE

I had just gotten out of the hospital gown and into some clothes when I heard a knock on the hospital door. "Come in," I said.

The female officer from the last time I was in the hospital entered followed behind Maddie. "A little birdie told me you were here," Officer Parish said.

"That little birdie's name wouldn't happen to be Sade, now would it?" I asked, although I already knew the answer.

"Well, it wouldn't be a little birdie if I told you," the officer responded.

All three of us laughed. Officer Parish asked, "Seriously, Ms. Washington. How are you?"

"I've been better, but nothing like the last time."

"I heard it was an accident, but what I'm concerned about is what happened before the accident."

I looked at Maddie and then back at Officer Parish. "We were arguing about something and the next thing I know we were being hit."

Maddie said, "You can save your breath. She's not going to turn on him."

Officer Parish asked, "Did you read any of those pamphlets?"

"I didn't have time," I lied. I did not intend to read them. I was living the life mentioned in those pamphlets and didn't feel the need to read about it.

"I understand he's right down the hall. I can have him escorted straight to the police station. All we need is a statement from you," Officer Parish eagerly said.

I didn't have the heart to be the cause of another black man going to jail. "I just can't do it. As much as I'm upset at Calvin right now, he's still my husband." I looked at Maddie. "Maddie, I'm ready to go."

The officer and Maddie both looked disappointed, but I couldn't concern myself with pleasing them. I'm the one who has to live with my decision. I didn't want to be the reason why Calvin was behind bars. Besides, he would only call me for bail money and then I would be out of money. No. I would deal with my problems with Calvin on my own and outside of the legal system.

Maddie took me home. I thanked her and enjoyed peace in the house at least another day because Calvin hadn't been discharged from the hospital yet. Sade insisted on staying home from school to help me out.

"You could have gone to school. I'm okay," I said as Sade plumped up a pillow and placed it under my head while I laid on the couch.

"I didn't feel like going."

"Nothing's wrong with the baby is there?" I asked. She was close to her due date and I'm sure all of this stress wasn't good for her or the baby.

"No. Just tired. I don't know if I'll be able to carry this baby to term mama. My back hurts. My legs hurt. My whole body hurts."

I didn't mean to laugh, but couldn't resist. Sade didn't find anything funny. "Baby girl, welcome to motherhood. It'll get worse before it gets better."

"Ugh," Sade groaned. She plopped down in the chair.

"Don't worry. You got your mama here to walk you through the rest of your pregnancy."

Sade didn't seem to be reassured. She flipped from station to station and then stopped on the music video station. "That's my song there."

"Speaking of songs. When can I hear one of your songs? You've yet to let me hear one."

"I didn't think you were interested."

I shifted on the couch. "I'm always interested in what you're doing. Mama just didn't have much time with work and things, but now that I've been fired, all I have is time."

"Fired? What happened?"

"It's not important. We'll be all right. I got six months of pay and it's not going to take me six months to find another job. I'm hoping I get one quick and then I can use the money for a nice down payment on something for us."

"As long as HE's not going, then I'm cool with that."

I didn't have the energy to discuss Calvin with Sade. I changed the subject to Brandon. "Brandon's a special young man. I hope you realize that."

"I hope he never changes."

I remembered being young and in love. Now I was older and in a messed up situation. I loved Calvin, but if truth be told, I was falling out of love with him. I zoned out while Sade talked about Brandon.

My mind drifted to the woman who boldly stepped to me in Calvin's hospital room. I wondered how long Calvin and Lisa had been messing around. It was obvious from the woman's response that she knew about me. It's one thing when the woman doesn't know about the wife, but when the woman knows and tries to act like she's the main woman, the other woman needed to get her assed kicked. That's what upset me the most. This woman knew. I wanted to whoop her behind from the front of the hospital to the back.

And that Calvin. He sat in the bed all smug. Since I've been discharged from the hospital, Calvin's been

blowing up my cell phone with calls and texts, but I refused to talk to him. I don't know when he's being released. When he does, he can find his own way home. In fact, he needed to call Lisa.

"Mama, are you going to call the landlord so we can get the locks changed?" Sade repeated herself.

"Sade, this thing between Calvin and I is our business. I got this. You just worry about you and that baby."

I felt bad for my tone of voice, but how could I tell Sade what my plans were, when I had no clue on where I wanted to go from here. Things couldn't go back to how they were, but still at this point, I had no plans.

~48~

I was sitting on the couch chatting with Brandon on the phone when I heard a knock on the door. "Brandon, let me call you back. Somebody's at the door." I placed my phone on the couch and went to the front door. "Who is it?"

"Sade, open up the door. It's me," Calvin said from the other side of the front door.

I didn't know if I should. My mom hadn't told me not to let Calvin back in, so reluctantly; I unlocked the bottom lock and then the deadbolt.

"Bout time," Calvin said, bursting through the door, barely giving me time to move out the way.

"Mama's sleeping," I said, hoping he would keep the noise down.

"She needs to wake up and tell me why I had to find another way home. I waited two hours and if it wasn't for my boy Mike, I would have had to catch the bus."

I snickered. "Well, it's not like she had a way to pick you up. Because of you, her car is totaled."

"Oh, you think it's funny huh." Calvin turned from where he stood and the look on his face caused me to stop in my tracks.

Maybe I had crossed the line. I didn't want him to try to attack me and harm my baby, so I tried to play it off and said, "Can't you take a joke."

"Ain't nothing funny." Calvin stomped away to his room.

I sighed. Now that Calvin was back, I didn't feel like being in the living room. I grabbed my cell phone off the couch and went to my room. I wrote a quick diary entry about Brandon and then eased the diary back under my mattress.

I undressed and got in bed. I was not only physically exhausted, but also mentally exhausted. It didn't take me long to drift into sleep. At first I thought I was dreaming when I felt lips kissing my chest, but the moment I realized I had forgotten to lock my door, I knew I wasn't dreaming. This was real and now I was fully awake and scared. My eyes flew open and saw Calvin in my personal space.

"Shhh. Don't move," Calvin's voice said.

I pushed him. "Mama! Mama!"

"Your mom's sleep," Calvin said and went back to groping me.

"Calvin, please get off me. I beg you," I whimpered. All I could think about was my unborn child. I didn't want to fall of the bed and hurt my baby, but I had to get Calvin off me.

Calvin used his hand and brushed my bang away from my face. "You're so cute when you try to resist. You're having my baby and I want to feel you. Now come on. It won't take long."

"No, please don't do this. Calvin, this isn't right. You know it," I said. "It ain't right," I said repeatedly.

Calvin slapped me. "Didn't I tell you to shut up?"

I screamed out. My face stung as tears fell down my face. I was tired of being the victim. I mustered up as much strength as I could and fought with all of my might to get Calvin off me.

He was stronger and every time it seemed like I was getting loose, Calvin was able to pen me back down. "The more you fight, the more exciting it is for me," he said.

"You're evil. I can't see what my mama sees in you." I cried.

"Well, if you hadn't run Lisa off, I wouldn't have to do this. Now, I need some release and you, Sade, are going to give it to me."

I wouldn't give up. I fought, but it didn't do any good. Gone was the little girl who was afraid to scream out. I shouted as loud as I could. "Help! Somebody help me!"

"Nobody's coming to your rescue, so you might as well shut up." Calvin stood over me.

Maybe Calvin was right. My mom probably took another one of her sleeping pills. I closed my eyes and waited for the inevitable.

Pow! Pow!

My eyes snapped open when I heard the gunshots. Calvin's body seemed to be moving in slow motion as it fell to the floor. My mom stood in the doorway with a gun aimed at Calvin. The two bullets she fired hit him in the back.

"That'll be the last time you will touch my daughter, you lying bastard!" my mom yelled.

Her and my eyes locked. She walked and stood over Calvin. She kicked him. Calvin groaned in pain. He moaned, "I can't believe you shot me."

"I can't believe I believed your lies. All of this time. Right under my nose, you've been molesting my daughter."

"It's not what you think. She came on to me. Things haven't been going too well with us. I'm a man. Can you blame me?" Calvin blurted.

Tears streamed down my mom's face. Her eyes were blood shot red. She aimed the gun at Calvin's head. "I took up for you. I married you. I almost lost my daughter because of you."

"Joyce, baby. We can talk this out. Put the gun down," Calvin said.

Without taking her eyes off Calvin, she responded, "I don't want to hear anything you have to say."

As I watched the whole scene transpire, I grabbed my robe and put it on. I went to stand next to my mom. She was scaring me. I was afraid she was going to shoot Calvin in the head. "Mama, he's not worth it."

My mom held the gun, but her hand was shaky. With the gun still aimed at him, she turned and looked at me. "Baby, I'm sorry I didn't believe you when you tried to tell me about this monster."

I had mixed emotions right now, but I believed her when she said she was sorry. I just wished she would have believed me sooner. I tried to assure her things would be okay. "Mama, that's okay. It's all right now. He'll never hurt me again."

She looked at me and then down at Calvin. "I know he won't. He'll never hurt you, me, or another person again."

My mom let go of the trigger, but instead of bullet being released, the gun jammed up. Calvin laughed. "Don't you know you can't get rid of me?"

She kicked him in the chest. Calvin coughed. My mom shouted, "Shut the hell up."

While Joyce was trying to figure out what was wrong with the gun, I grabbed my cell phone and searched for my backpack. It wasn't in the room so it could only be in one other place. I left my mom

alone with Calvin. The backpack was right there by the couch where I left it. I dumped the contents of the backpack on the living room table until I saw what I was looking for. I found the card with Officer Parish's contact information and dialed her cell phone number. After making her realize who I was, I said, "Can you come? We need you right away." I walked back to my room. I stood in the doorway as me and Officer Parish talked.

"What happened?" Officer Parish asked.

"Calvin tried to rape me and my mama shot him in self defense."

"I'm on my way. Don't call anyone else. I'll handle this," Officer Parish assured me.

"Sade, you shouldn't have done that," my mom said.

"Mama, he's not worth it. Come on. The police will be here. We can tell them everything and we can finally be rid of him."

I looked at Calvin who was crunched up on the floor in the blood that had seeped from his body. He groaned as pain ripped through his body. Calvin reached out towards me when I walked by him. I kicked his hand away. "Die already."

~49~

JOYCE

I sat down on Sade's bed. My hand was shaking as I placed the gun down next to me. Calvin reached out to me. "Call nine-one-one," he cried out.

"I don't have a phone near me," I responded.

Calvin yelled, "Please, Joyce. My back is hurting. I can't move."

My body shook as I spoke. "Do you think I care? After all the shit you've done to my daughter."

"I'm sorry Joyce. Just call the ambulance, please."

"I'm not calling nobody. You can bleed to death as far as I'm concerned."

"Joyce, come on. Baby, I'm hurting." Calvin laid flat on his back in the pool of blood. I could tell he was in pain by the sound of his voice and the pained look on his face.

I blinked my eyes a few times. "Does it look like I care?"

"I'm sorry. I didn't mean for things to happen. It just happened."

"Running out of bath tissue just happens. Sleeping with your woman's daughter, no, doesn't just happen. You got to have a sick perverted mind to do what you did."

"It's not what you think, Joyce. Just hear me out." Calvin groaned.

Calvin's body curled up in pain. Seeing him in pain didn't move me to help him.

I was angry with him and angry with myself for not recognizing that I allowed a monster around my daughter all of these years. "I trusted you. I trusted my baby girl around you. You stole her innocence. You've ruined my little girl's life."

"It's not as bad as you make it out to be," Calvin managed to say.

I had enough. Before I realized it, I had stood up and spat on Calvin. "Calvin, are you serious? You've been raping my little girl."

"Don't say that." Calvin looked up at me.

"It's what you did. Now she's going to have to live with it for the rest of her life. And me." I was losing strength in my body so I sat back down on the bed. "She told me and I took up for you. What kind of mother does that make me?"

Calvin's cold black eyes stared back at me. "You knew. How could you have not known?"

"I didn't know anything?" I shook my head back and forth.

284

SPARKLE

"You mentioned the foul odor coming from Sade's room on more than one occasion, so don't go trying to fool yourself. You knew. You were just in denial," Calvin said.

I rocked myself back and forth as I listened to Calvin. He's right. I recalled smelling the odor, but it never dawned on me it was because of my little girl and my man having sex. Instead of answering his questions, I said, "I hope you rot in hell for the things you've done to my girl."

"You'll be right there with me for being a rotten mom."

Calvin's words cut me to the core. I should have paid closer attention to Sade, but most importantly, when Sade told me that Calvin was her baby's daddy, I should have believed her. But instead of believing her, I was hell bent on proving Sade wrong.

I'm fortunate that Sade really didn't mean she hated me. That she only told me that out of anger. Fortunately, Sade never turned her back on me, even when I hadn't been a good mom to her. I cried and the tears blinded me. Through blurry eyes, I watched Calvin squirm around on the floor. The sight of him made me want to crush his face in with my bare foot.

Calvin had fooled me with his pretty boy smile and smooth talking ways. Others hinted to me about Calvin being a user and womanizer, but I never wanted to believe it. I took Calvin for his word, but

Calvin wasn't a man of honor. I worked long hours to keep a roof over our heads and food on the table, while Calvin had it on easy street. Over and over, I made excuse after excuse for why Calvin wouldn't go out and do what most real men would do--take care of their families. The time Calvin had stolen from me couldn't be gotten back. Calvin ruined two lives; three lives because that included Sade's unborn child.

A moment of epiphany took my mind back to when I should have suspected Calvin's treacherous behavior started. The day I came home from working the graveyard shift and saw the blood on Sade's sheets. No wonder it was three years before Sade actually started her period.

I felt a panic attack coming on. I took a few deep breaths to control my breathing. What if I hadn't heard Sade's cries while I slept earlier? The sound of Sade's cries jolted me out of my sleep. I retrieved the gun Maddie had given me when she stopped by earlier. I had hidden in a box and had placed it under my bed. When I heard Sade scream, I grabbed it out of the box and rushed to Sade's room.

When I saw Calvin standing over Sade, I snapped. I didn't think twice about it. I immediately pulled the trigger and the bullets pierced Calvin in the back. If he didn't fall when he did, I would have shot several more rounds. The sight of him about to rape my pregnant daughter was enough to make anyone snap in my opinion. I kept scanning my mind for memories. Tried to figure out what clues were left that I overlooked while this happened right under my nose.

Angry and disgusted, I asked, "I want to know why, Calvin. Why my daughter? Why hurt her? Why hurt me?"

"I don't know, Joyce. I'm sorry. I didn't mean to hurt Sade."

I threw a pillow off the bed at Calvin. "Don't ever mention her name again."

"I really am sorry."

Nothing Calvin said made sense to me now. I didn't want to hear it. I picked up the gun off the bed and aimed it at Calvin's head. I hoped it was no longer jammed because I wanted to put Calvin down for good and maybe, just maybe, the pain I was feeling would go away.

"Mom, don't," Sade walked in the room and said, just in time.

~50~

SADE

O fficer Parish walked in behind me and said, "Ms. Washington, put the gun down. He's not worth you going to jail over."

"Oh, she's going to jail for shooting me," Calvin yelled.

"Mama, please. I need you here with me. Put the gun down."

"I'm sorry baby. I didn't know. I really didn't know." my mom cried as she eased the gun down.

I ran up to her and we hugged and cried.

Officer Parish used her attached walkie-talkie and said, "We need an ambulance. I'm in Fair Parks Heights. Apartment two sixteen."

My mom asked, "Am I under arrest?" My mom held on to my arm.

"No, but he is for trying to rape your daughter." Officer Parish read Calvin his Miranda Rights. "You have the right to remain silent. Anything you say can and will be held against you in court."

SPARKLE

While Officer Parish was dealing with Calvin, I said to my mama, "I'm scared mama." I knew I had just turned sixteen, but I felt like the scared little ten-year-old from six years ago.

Officer Parish motioned for us to follow her out the room. We did as we were told. Officer Parish said, "I should have called for backup and paramedics when Sade called me, but I didn't because I wanted to check out the seriousness of the situation first." She looked at my mom. "Although I don't condone what you did, as a woman and a mother, I understand why you did it."

"But what if the other officers arrest me? What's going to happen to Sade?"

"If you two trust me, you both will be here tonight. But you got to trust me, okay?" Officer Parish asked.

My mom responded, "We'll do whatever you like."

I shook my head in agreement.

Officer Parish said, "I want you to both agree that I happened to stop by because you were ready to give me a statement about Calvin. I just happen to show up when you caught him trying to rape Sade."

"Calvin's going to say something different. I know it," my mom said.

"Nobody is going to believe him because it'll be three of us saying the same thing verses him. Calvin can say what he wants, but he's going to the hospital and when he gets out, he's going straight to jail."

289

"Without me there to support him. He's on his own," my mom said.

Officer Parish said to us, "Have a seat and rest your nerves. In a few minutes this place is going to be swarmed with police and probably news media too."

I looked at my mom. "I don't want to talk to anybody."

She said to me, "You must because they need to know I shot him to protect you."

The rage and pain from over the years rose out of me. In a harsh voice, I said, "Mama, you were a little late. Look at the results of him doing this to me."

"Baby, I'm so sorry. If I would have known, I would have let you get an abortion."

"That's just it. I told you he was the daddy and you wouldn't believe me. You took his word over mine. How do you think that made me feel?"

She looked away in shame. "I don't know what to say."

"You were there this time, but how about all of those other times when I needed you. When my eyes pled for you to help me."

"Why didn't you tell me? I would have stopped him then."

"Calvin threatened to kill you. I loved you mama. I still do. Even when you didn't care enough for me to protect me, I still loved you."

SPARKLE

I let the tears fall down my face. My mom cried too. We ended up holding each other, as the years of pain and guilt released itself through our tears. Knocks were heard at the door. Officer Parish opened the door and showed the paramedics where Calvin was and she took the lead with talking to her colleagues.

Two plain-clothes detectives wanted to talk to me alone, while another detective interviewed my mother. I made sure I stuck with the script. I repeated to them the exact same thing Officer Parish had told me to say. One of the detectives asked me, "Was this the first time he tried to attack you?"

It was hard for me to revisit that space in time. I could no longer look in the detectives face. My mom returned where I was seated I and squeezed her hand. "It's okay, baby. Tell them. Tell them so you can be free of that monster."

I took a deep breath. My eyes glossed over as my mind drifted back to the time it all started. I shared with them when it began and why I never told. By the time I was through telling the story, there was not a dry eye in the room.

The detective said, "I assure you that we're going to prosecute him to the fullest. Ms. Washington, don't worry about a thing. You protected your daughter. I don't see the DA filing any charges against you."

I sighed with relief. Calvin had taken so much from me. To hear the detective say my mom wouldn't be arrested helped me relax just a little. When the officers got ready to leave, I saw a few of the local media outside the door.

One of the reporters was heard saying, "We just want to talk to the mama. Mr. Thomas gave an interview. We want to get the wife's story."

Officer Parish said, "I got this."

My mom seemed relieved. Neither one of us was up for talking to the media. Officer Parish walked out of the apartment and faced the media in the hallway.

I sat down beside my mom on the couch as she turned the television to the twenty-four hours news station. We watched in amazement the live broadcast held right outside of our apartment. Even with all of the chaos outside, I finally felt like there was a sense of order in my life--with Calvin gone, my nightmare was finally over.

~51~

JOYCE

I cringed when I saw Calvin holler out to the reporter. "I'm a victim and they are trying to make me out to be some monster. The mother's crazy and the daughter is too."

"He's such a liar," Sade said.

Officer Parish answered a few questions from the reporters. "Mr. Thomas is being charged with indecency with a child, statutory rape, and assault. If you have any other questions, please filter them to Detective Jenkins. He'll be handling this case. Thank you for respecting the family as they deal with this difficult situation."

I turned in the direction of the front door as Officer Parish walked in. She looked at us and said, "Ladies, if you're all squared away here, I'll be going."

I got up and walked up to her. "Thank you for everything. I don't think I would have been able to get through these last few hours if you hadn't showed up when you did."

"Told you, I've been there." Officer Parish looked at Sade. "You take care of yourself and that baby of yours."

"Yes, ma'am," Sade responded.

"I'm about to go home to my kids and my new husband. Yes, I got a good man this time." Officer Parish whispered to me. "Don't waddle in self-pity. You said you didn't know, but now that you do, just make sure you do the right thing from this day forward. We all make mistakes."

"But look at my baby girl. How could I have not known?" I asked.

"I don't have the answers, but I do know that we can't change the past. I'm going to keep you in my prayers."

I did what came naturally and hugged Officer Parish. "May God bless you."

Officer Parish left. I locked both of the locks on the front door. My phone rang off the hook. By now, most people I knew had seen the newscasts on at least one of the television stations. After Maddie called three times in a row, I picked up.

"Calvin, couldn't go away quietly, he wanted to bring shame on us even more," I told Maddie. Frustrated and upset that Calvin turned on me so quick.

"I'm just glad you finally got rid of him, but girl, did you have to shoot him?" Maddie laughed.

I laughed too. "If it was up to me, he would have been going out of here in a body bag, but the plea in Sade's eyes is what stopped me from pulling the trigger and shooting him in the head."

"I'm glad you didn't because he's not worth you spending the rest of your life in prison. He'll now get everything he deserves."

I ended the call with Maddie. Sadie was fast asleep on the couch. I retrieved a blanket from the hallway closet and wrapped it over Sade's body. I was tired, but couldn't rest. Calvin's imprint was all over this place; especially our bedroom. I went to the kitchen, got trash bags, and started filling the bags up with Calvin's stuff.

Calvin's cell phone kept beeping. I picked it up off the dresser and scanned it. I saw several text messages from various people. Some seemed to be women he was messing with. "Lisa, looks like he was playing you too," I said.

I was about to toss it in the bag with his other stuff, but decided to keep it just in case I needed it to give to the police. I don't know where my extra energy came from, but I didn't stop until I had all I could find of Calvin's stuff in the bags. I knew it was too early in the morning to be calling anyone, but I didn't care. I dialed Michael, Calvin's friend. He was sleep, but when he realized it was me, he talked. "Joyce, I heard

about what happened. Is there anything I can do?"
Michael sleepily asked.

"Yes, please come by here in the morning and get
your boys stuff out of my house."

"What do you want me to do with it?" he asked.

"Burn it for all I care. I just need it out."

"Okay. I'll bring some of our friends and help move
it."

"And Mike?" I said.

"Yes."

"Do you know where I can hawk some jewelry?"

"I got you. I'll get it sold and bring you the money,"
Michael assured me.

"You can keep it or better yet, donate it to a
women's shelter in Calvin's memory."

I pulled the comforter and both sheets off the bed
and threw them in a trash bag. "I never liked that
comforter anyway."

I put some clean sheets on the bed and retrieved a
blanket out of the closet. I laid down, but sleep
escaped me. I grabbed the blanket off the bed and
went to sit in the living room chair so I could keep an
eye on Sade.

I watched Sade sleep. She looked so peaceful. I
cried as I thought about how Calvin stole Sade's
innocence from her. I blamed myself and regardless
of what anyone else said, I would go to my grave
blaming myself.

~52~
SADE

The couch wasn't normally the best place to sleep, but it had been the best rest I'd had in years. When I woke up, I was surprised to see my mom fast asleep in the chair.

My bladder wouldn't let me sit so I rushed to the bathroom. When I returned to the living room, my mom was folding up the blankets.

"Oh, I could have done that," I said.

"No, baby. You've been through enough. Sit. You and the baby need to rest."

"I'm fine," I assured her.

After folding up the blankets, she sat next to me on the couch and we watched the morning news. I asked, "Mom, what's going to happen next? Will they let Calvin out on bail? Do you think we should be scared that he's going to try to come back and do something to us?"

"No, baby. He's going to be in the hospital for a while. I just heard on the news that the doctors think he's going to be paralyzed. The bullets pierced his spinal cord."

"Wow. That's payback for real."

"I don't feel any remorse whatsoever. You saved his life because I was ready to pull the trigger," she said.

"I couldn't lose you too."

In my mind, my mom had been lost to me for these past six years. I didn't want to lose her to the penitentiary so I didn't save Calvin because of any sort of compassion for him. My reasons were selfish-- I wanted to save my mom from ending her life.

"I need a shower. I'll be back," I told my mom.

When I exited the bathroom twenty minutes later, my mom met me in the hallway and said, "You have company."

Crystal, Dena, and Brandon were all seated in the living room. Brandon didn't wait for me to reach the couch. He jumped up and quickly embraced me in his arms. I felt protected.

"Don't you all supposed to be in school?" I asked as Brandon released me.

"Our best friend just went through an ordeal, school can wait," Dena said.

Brandon helped me to the couch. "Why didn't you call me?" he asked.

"Stuff just happened so fast. The police was here. By the time everybody left, I was exhausted."

"I bet," Crystal said.

"So what happened?" Dena crossed her legs under her and leaned forward so she wouldn't miss hearing anything.

I gave them the condensed version. Brandon remained quiet. I wondered what was going through his mind when I admitted that Calvin was the father of my unborn child.

My two besties were just glad that I was fine. I asked Dena, "What did you want last night? With everything going on, I didn't have a chance to return your text."

Dena said, "We might be signing a record deal soon. Jada got a call from one of the record executives yesterday."

I was happy, but with all that had transpired over the last twenty-four hours, I couldn't muster up the excitement I'm sure Crystal and Dena felt. "That would be great. I hope it works out."

Crystal's cell phone rang. "Well, my mom's downstairs," Crystal said after looking at her cell phone.

I said, "Thanks for checking on me. I love you guys."

"We love you too," Crystal walked over and hugged me.

Dena followed suit and hugged me too. "I'm riding with Crystal, so I got to jet too."

"I'll call y'all later." I watched them leave.

"I had no idea you were going through all that," Brandon said as soon as Crystal and Dena left out of the apartment.

"It's not something that I like to talk about."

"But we share everything. I thought you felt comfortable talking to me about everything."

I could see the pain in Brandon's eyes. "Brandon, I do. It's just that I was embarrassed. Thought you wouldn't want anything else to do with me."

Brandon picked up my hand. "I love you, Sade. It's my job to protect you. I knew you didn't like him. If I knew he had been putting his hands on you, I would have shot him myself."

I squeezed his hand. "It's good to know you have my back."

My mom walked in the room and said, "Brandon thanks for being there for Sade. I'm glad she at least had you to turn to."

"I love her Ms. Joyce."

"I know you do. Well, I'm going to go talk to the apartment manager." She looked around the room and said, "We will not be spending another night in this place."

Good, I thought.

Brandon asked, "Do you need me to stay?"

"No, she's just going downstairs. I'll be okay. I got you, right?" I said, nervously. I was hoping my revelation didn't push him away.

"You won't get rid of me that easy," Brandon assured me.

Brandon kissed me on the forehead and left me alone in the apartment. I smiled, closed, and locked the door behind him. I looked around the apartment. Now that Calvin was out of our lives, my mom and I could get back to living. I've been living a nightmare since the day my mom let Calvin move in. I hadn't had a peaceful night of sleep since the day Calvin raped me. Even though I had put the locks on my door, I didn't sleep peacefully because my dreams would turn into nightmares.

I'd looked forward to this day. The day that Calvin Thomas wouldn't be a thorn in my side. The day that he would be away from my mother. The day I looked forward to getting my mom back. No matter what happened after today, I was confident that I would be just fine.

No, turning sixteen hadn't been sweet, but I now had something to look forward to a peaceful life. I rubbed my stomach and thought, "And a child to protect."

SADE'S SECRET:
A SWEET 16 DIARIES NOVEL

AUTHOR BIO

Sparkle is the pseudonym for Essence Magazine bestselling author Shelia M. Goss. Shelia is also the author of the young adult series, The Lip Gloss Chronicles. Besides writing young adult books, she writes books for adults. For more information, visit

www.sheliagoss.com

or

www.sheliagoss.com/sparklewrites

www.wcpyoungadult.com

READING GROUP QUESTIONS

1. Why do you think Sade kept a secret from her mom and friends for all of those years?
2. What would you have done in Sade's situation?
3. Do you know someone who has experienced something similar as Sade?
4. Why do you think Sade's mother Joyce ignored the signs that her boyfriend Calvin was molesting Sade?
5. Do you feel that Joyce suffered from low self-esteem?
6. When Joyce was confronted with the facts, she still didn't believe Sade. Do you think she knew the truth but ignored it? Why?
7. Do you feel Joyce is as much to blame about Sade's abuse as Calvin?
8. Do you think Joyce and Sade's relationship can be saved after going through such an ordeal?
9. Do you think Sade should have confided in someone else after her mother didn't believe her?
10. What emotions did you feel as you read Sade's story?

If you or someone you know is dealing with abuse please visit the Stop It Now website: http://www.stopitnow.org
or call 1-888-PREVENT

W·CLARK
PUBLISHING
60 Evergreen Place, Suite 904
East Orange New Jersey 07018

ATTENTION:

We are seeking submissions for the
Wahida Clark Presents Young Adult Line.

Submission Guidelines:

- ✓ No emailed submissions accepted.
- ✓ Submissions must be typed and double spaced.
- ✓ No handwritten submissions.

www.wcpyoungadult.com

WAHIDA CLARK PRESENTS

Y.A.
YOUNG ADULT

NINETY NINE
PROBLEMS

A Young Adult Novel BY
GLORIA DOTSON-LEWIS